SHOWING OFF

Also by Sarah Mlynowski, Lauren Myracle
& Emily Jenkins:

#1 Upside-Down Magic

#2 Sticks & Stones

UPSIDE ★ DOWN MAGIC

SHOWING OFF

by

Sarah
MLYNOWSKI,

Lauren
MYRACLE,

and

Emily
JENKINS

SCHOLASTIC PRESS/*New York*

Library of Congress Cataloging-in-Publication Data available

ISBN 978-0-545-80053-2

10 9 8 7 6 5 4 3 2 1   17 18 19 20 21 .

Printed in the U.S.A.   23
First edition, January 2017

Book design by Abby Dening

To Todd, Randy, and Daniel,
who deserve unicorn gummies, lemon drops,
and choco fire trucks.

Nory Horace arrived at Dunwiddle Magic
School with really wet feet.

It was late October and rain poured
down. The sky was dark even though it was morning.

Nory wore a raincoat.

She held an umbrella.

But she didn't have rain boots.

Back when Nory had lived with her father,
brother, and sister, she'd owned a shiny pair of orange
boots decorated with cheerful blue ducks. They were
really great boots.

But now she lived with Aunt Margo. And she had no boots.

How had Nory been separated from her rain boots? She had flunked the Big Test to get into Sage Academy, that's how.

Sage Academy was the fancy private magic school where Nory's father was the headmaster. When Nory had flunked the Big Test, Father was so upset, he sent Nory away. She had moved to the town of Dunwiddle to live with Aunt Margo so she could go to a public school with a special new class for fifth graders who had wonky magic.

Of course, you weren't supposed to say *wonky*. The word *wonky* was rude. You were supposed to say *different* or *unusual*.

See, Nory was a Fluxer. That was her magic talent. Magic talents bubbled up when a person was around ten. Once you started fifth grade at magic school, you studied one of the five Fs of the magical world.

Fluxers were one of the five Fs. They could turn into animals.

Flyers flew.

Flares had fire magic.

Fuzzies had animal magic.

Flickers had invisibility magic of one sort or another.

Usually, Fluxers turned into ordinary animals like cats, dogs, cows, and goats. But Nory Horace didn't flux like that. Nory fluxed into mixed-up animals. When she did, she often lost control of her human mind. The animal mind took over.

It was very embarrassing.

Nory had been able to hide her problems for a bit. But during the Big Test to get into Sage Academy, she had fluxed into a snake-kitten in front of a lot of Very Important People.

Then Snitten-Nory had unhinged her snake jaw and chomped on her own father's hand, because it happened to smell like salmon.

Afterward, she turned into a dragon-kitten.

And she might have breathed a little fire.

Or a lot of fire.

And she might have zoomed around the testing room in an inappropriate way.

Okay, she did do that. Nory *did* turn into a dritten, and she *did* do all those things—and some things that were even worse.

It had been very, very humiliating.

She didn't like to think about it. And since Father didn't like to think about it either, he had shipped her off to live with Aunt Margo, as soon as arrangements could be made.

Nory hadn't packed her rain boots when she moved, because she'd been in a state of shock. When a person is thinking, *My whole life is falling apart! My magic is so wonky that my dad is ashamed of me! I have to move to a new town! Where I won't know anyone! I'll be stuck in a class of wonkos just like me, only wonkier!* that person doesn't also think, *Oh, hmm, in October it'll be rainy, probably. I'll pack my rain boots.*

Now here she was, six weeks into the school year at Dunwiddle. It was the first day of serious rain and her feet were *soaked*. But what was a girl to do? Wet feet were wet feet. Nothing was gained by moping.

Nory was good at looking on the bright side. It helped that she'd walked to school with her new best friend, Elliott. "Do you have extra shoes in your locker?" Elliott asked as they stepped through the entrance.

Everyone in Nory's Upside-Down Magic class kept extra clothes at school. They needed them. One of their classmates, Willa Ingeborg, had Upside-Down Flare magic that created indoor rain, and not always on purpose.

The students got wet pretty often.

Nory looked inside her locker. Bummer. She didn't have extra shoes, but she *did* have an extra pair of red socks. "Oh well, I can spend the day in socks," she told Elliott as she put them on.

"But the floor's a mess," he pointed out. "You'll

get them wet." His ice magic wouldn't help, Nory figured. Elliott was an Upside-Down Flare. He could freeze things. But a frozen floor would be worse than a wet floor. Everyone would slip. "Wait!" Elliott cried. "I have a better idea! Be right back!"

Nory stood still. Around her, students came in, closing up their umbrellas and hanging their raincoats in their lockers. All of them wore rain boots. A couple of Flyers hovered a foot or so off the ground to avoid the puddles, even though there was no flying allowed in the hallways.

Less than a minute later, Elliott returned with the wheelbarrow. The UDM kids usually used it to bring Bax Kapoor to the nurse's office. Bax was an Upside-Down Fluxer who accidentally turned into a rock almost every day.

"Hop in!" Elliott said.

Nory rode to class with her head propped in her hands and her legs dangling over the edge. Her feet felt cozy and dry in her red socks.

I may be down a pair of rain boots, she thought, *but I'm definitely up in friends.*

Dunwiddle Magic School was fifth through eighth grades. The students were divided into the five magic categories: Flares, Flyers, Flickers, Fluxers, and Fuzzies. Then there was group of unusual kids like Nory: the fifth-grade Upside-Down Magic kids. Those kids studied with Ms. Starr, the Upside-Down Magic teacher. Ms. Starr taught literature, social studies, gym, math, and science—and she also had special training to help kids with upside-down magic. She wanted them to get in touch with their unusual talents. They did headstands in class. They hula-hooped. They did interpretive dance (though none of them liked it). They did trust exercises. They tried to feel their emotions and channel their magical talents productively.

Today, after math, Nory slid her protractor into her desk. Her friend Andres Padillo was floating on the ceiling, attached to a long leash connected to his belt, as usual. Andres was an Upside-Down Flyer. He'd flown up, up, up on the day his magic came in, and *he had never flown down.* That's why he had to be on a leash. He couldn't stop flying.

Nory had an idea she'd been wanting to try. "Pull Andres down," she told Elliott. "Hey, Andres! Let's do a gravity experiment. I'm going to sit on you, okay?"

Marigold Ramos came over. "We're going to sit on Andres?"

"I'm not sure about this," muttered Andres as Elliott reeled him down.

"You'll be fine!" Nory said. "It's for science!" To Marigold, she added in a whisper, "Don't shrink him."

Marigold wasn't an upside-down talent. Or at least, no one had ever been able to put a label on her magic. She shrank things, but she couldn't make them big again afterward.

Andres was now floating level with the desks. He

grabbed on to the back of a chair with one hand and on to Elliott's shirt with the other. Elliott struggled with the leash, trying to keep him low. Andres's feet kept floating up.

Nory hopped onto a chair. She pulled Marigold up with her. "I'll sit on his shoulders. Marigold, you sit on his back. And, Andres, we're going to try to weigh you down. But maybe you'll fly us up, instead. Either way will be excellent, okay?"

"You might hit your heads on the ceiling," warned Andres.

"Students!" Ms. Starr said, walking over. "What in the world is going on?"

"An experiment, Ms. Starr," said Andres. Nory and Marigold were sitting on him, but he hadn't lowered down to the floor. He was just about two feet off the ground, with Elliott still holding the leash tightly.

"Girls, there will be no riding of Andres."

"But it's a *science* experiment," said Marigold.

"Yes," Nory said. "We're learning about gravity!"

Ms. Starr made her mouth into a stern shape. "Gravity is very interesting," she said, "but friends do not ride friends. Not even if you have permission. You all know that about Fluxers, right? You don't ride your fluxed classmates. And you don't ride your Flyer classmates either. So please. Marigold, Nory, Elliott. Let Andres go."

Nory and Marigold climbed off Andres, reluctantly. Elliott released the leash slowly and Andres bobbed back up to the ceiling. "Sorry, Andres," Nory called as her friend steadied himself against the top of a bookshelf.

Andres was laughing too hard to reply.

"Listen up," said Ms. Starr. "Today, for our magic studies, we are going to foot paint."

"Foot painting!" Nory wondered aloud. "Is that like finger painting?"

"It's good for managing new sensory input and creativity at the same time," Ms. Starr said. "That's an important skill for kids with unusual magic. Nory, will you and Pepper go to the art room? Bring back four jars of poster paint, please. The big plastic jars. You can pick the colors."

Pepper Phan was tiny. She had jet-black pigtails and a round, friendly face. Pepper was an Upside-Down Fuzzy. More specifically, she was a Fierce.

Typical Fuzzies tamed unicorns or commanded groups of rabbits. Some sent carrier pigeons, or swam with alligators. Pepper was the opposite. Instead of trusting her, animals feared her.

Unfortunately, she couldn't turn her magic off. All animals, even people fluxed into animal form, thought Pepper was a terrifying monster.

When Nory was human, she liked Pepper a lot. Pepper was thoughtful and kept candy in her pockets. They both liked to hide out in the Dunwiddle supply closet when school got stressful.

Now the two of them walked down the hall together. The floor had dried. Bright red fire extinguishers lined the walls in case of Flare problems. The neatly printed signs read:

NO FLYING EXCEPT IN THE FLYERS' COURT OR THE YARD.

NO ANIMAL FRIENDS IN SCHOOL WITHOUT WRITTEN
PERMISSION.

NO FLUXING WITHOUT TEACHER SUPERVISION.

Today, Nory noticed a sign she had never bothered to read before. It read:

DO NOT RIDE ON YOUR FELLOW STUDENTS.

They passed the fifth-grade Flyer class. Kids were at their desks, levitating slightly above their seats. The teacher was shaking a maraca, saying, "Up two-three-four, down two-three-four." The students raised and lowered themselves by magic.

"I'm glad I'm not a Flyer," said Nory. "Their lessons are so boring."

They passed the invisible water fountain and the signs for next week's kittenball games and invisible diving competitions. They stepped up to the art room.

The door was closed, so Nory knocked twice.

"Come in!" someone called.

They went in.

Suddenly, Pepper clutched Nory's arm. "Oh, no."

"What?" Nory asked.

Pepper was frozen in place.

Nory's eyes followed Pepper's. The kids in the art room were eighth-grade Fluxers. Most of them were in human form, but in the back of the room sat an elephant. She held a pencil in her trunk. It was Andres's sister, Carmen. She'd won a fluxing award for being able to do such an advanced animal. No one else in eighth grade could do any kind of large mammal yet.

The art teacher, Mr. Hamil, was also a Fluxer. He sat in the center of a large table, posing while the students drew. His elbows were on his knees. His chin was in his palms.

He was in the form of a chimpanzee.

One elephant plus one chimpanzee equaled two jungle animals, and that was bad news for Pepper the Fierce.

2

Pepper knew from experience that fierced animals get even more frightened if she moved. Maybe things would be okay if she just stood still?

But no. It was starting. She felt scared and slippery inside. That was the best way to describe it. When her magic turned on, something shifted within her. Her stomach turned to Jell-O. Her skin felt slick. Her thoughts flew every which way.

A dangerous energy sparked, like static electricity, only spikier. Chimp-Hamil turned to look at Pepper. His eyes grew round.

"Eeee!" he screeched. "Eeee-eeee-eee!"

Twelve humans, one chimp, and one elephant swiveled their heads to see what was going on. Elephant-Carmen bellowed. (Fluxers couldn't speak when they were in animal form.)

Chimp-Hamil clacked his ape teeth and leapt onto the shoulders of an eighth-grade boy.

"What the zum-zum?" the boy shrieked. "Mr. Hamil, you're choking me!"

"He looks like he might bite!" a girl cried. "Jamie, you have to get out of there! Flux into something small!"

The boy immediately fluxed into a hamster. Then Hamster-Jamie and Chimp-Hamil crashed to the floor, knocking over several jars of paint as they fell.

"Zwingo!" cried another boy. "Has Mr. Hamil lost his human mind?"

"Where's Jamie?" asked the loud girl who'd told him to flux.

From beneath Chimp-Hamil, Hamster-Jamie screamed.

"The teacher's squishing him!" Nory cried. "He's trapped!"

One of the girls said, "Flux into something that can stop Mr. Hamil!"

"No! Don't flux at all!" shouted Pepper.

But—

Pop-pop-pop!

Three of the eighth graders fluxed. One turned into a pit bull, one into a boxer, and one into a gorilla. The gorilla was reaching for Chimp-Hamil when the dogs saw Pepper. Both of them barked their heads off, and the gorilla screamed a horrible ape scream.

"Pepper, no!" Nory cried.

Pepper turned to look at Nory. Only, what was going on? Nory's face looked like it had turned to wax. *Hot* wax. Her forehead bulged out. Then her forehead went back to normal, but her cheeks rippled. Nory was fluxing by accident.

"Nory, stop!" Pepper begged.

Nory seemed like she was trying to speak, but Pepper couldn't make out her words.

Pop-pop-pop!

Kitten body, kitten paws, kitten tail. Dragon claws, dragon wings, dragon teeth.

Nory was a dritten.

Dritten-Nory flapped into the air, yowling and breathing fire.

Pepper sidestepped the flames, and Dritten-Nory turned in midair. She flapped right out of the classroom, yowling all the way.

Pepper followed. She was heading for the door when a boy slammed it shut and moved a desk in front of it.

"It's not safe in the hall!" the boy cried. "There's a flaming dragon!"

Pepper was trapped. She squeezed her eyes shut and tried to turn off her Fierceness.

It didn't work. That was no surprise. She'd never been able to turn off her magic before. Pepper opened her eyes and faced the art room. "I'm just a fifth grader who came to get some paint for a project!" she yelled at the chaos. "I'm harmless!"

Elephant-Carmen reared back. Chimp-Hamil hooted and danced.

Elephant-Carmen trumpeted and rammed her front feet through the ground-floor classroom window. *Smash!* She jumped through the opening.

The dogs and the gorilla followed her lead.

Chimp-Hamil threw a jar of paint at Pepper. He had lost much of his human mind, but he appeared to be trying to protect his students as best he could. The jar broke on the floor and splattered everyone with green paint. He threw another, and yellow splattered. Hamster-Jamie scrabbled his legs and scurried to hide beneath a rolling cart.

"Stop!" Pepper yelled. "I'm not going to hurt you!"

Chimp-Hamil stopped. He looked around, eyes bugging out. Then he turned his back on Pepper and leapt out the broken window.

"Please just leave," the loud girl said to Pepper.

"I'm sorry! I'm not doing it on purpose!"

The loud girl shook her head. "Just go away before you make things worse!"

Arms shaking, Pepper pulled the desk out of the way.

The boy who had put it in place narrowed his eyes at her. "Your magic is really wonky," he said.

Pepper felt like sobbing, but she lifted her chin high and opened the door. "In case you didn't know, it's rude to call someone *wonky*."

She spun on her heel and fast-walked down the hall, blinking back tears.

When Pepper turned the corner, Nory stepped into view. She was back to being a human, thank goodness. "Pepper! Wait!" she called.

Pepper stopped.

Nory gestured at the place where the invisible water fountain stood. "I flew into the fountain. I must have pressed the lever by accident. But on the bright side, the cold water was such a shock, I fluxed back into me."

Pepper looked at Nory. Her hair had come out of

its ponytail on one side. Also, her shirt was wet. "Are you okay?"

"Yeah. I'm okay. Sorry about turning into a dritten. I nearly burned you."

"That's all right. Sorry about being a Fierce."

Nory took Pepper's hand. "I know you couldn't help it. Neither of us could."

At the main office, Nory and Pepper told Principal Gonzalez what had happened in the art room.

His eyebrows pulled together like unhappy caterpillars. He took a deep breath. He thanked them for letting him know.

He called the janitor. He called Coach Vitomin, Nory's tutor, who had experience with panicked Fluxers. He called Nurse Riley. Then he sent Pepper and Nory back to class and headed toward the art room.

Pepper and Nory took the long way around, to avoid passing the Fuzzy animal room.

"How's your tutoring going?" Nory asked as they walked.

Nory and Bax worked twice a week with Coach, since they were both Upside-Down Fluxers. The other kids in Ms. Starr's class also had tutors who helped them make the most of their upside-down powers. Even Marigold finally had a tutor now. The school had found a specialist from the nearby University of Maine, since her magic was so unusual.

Ms. Starr herself was Pepper's tutor because she, too, was an Upside-Down Fuzzy. Ms. Starr wasn't a Fierce like Pepper, though. Pepper didn't know what made Ms. Starr upside down, actually. Ms. Starr hadn't showed her magic at school yet, and she hadn't told the students exactly what it was.

"It's not going well," Pepper told Nory. "So far, all we do is nostril breathing and extra hula-hooping. Ms. Starr thinks those activities will balance my energy or something. But hello? Obviously not working very well."

When they arrived at the UDM classroom, they saw a ream of white paper spread across the floor. All the kids stood in bare feet. "Girls! Finally!" Ms. Starr exclaimed. Her smile faded, and she gave a puzzled blink. "I'm glad to see you. But where's the paint?"

They had some explaining to do.

3

Ms. Starr went to get the paint herself.

When she got back, she explained that the foot-painting activity was a way to "explore their roots," since feet were the rootiest part of the human body. "Magic is grounded in the feet," said Ms. Starr. "I want you to come alive to the sensations in your toes and heels. Make a connection between those feelings and artistic expression as you paint. We all know art and magic are connected!"

She climbed a ladder and taped paper on the ceiling for Andres. Sometimes he used backpacks of bricks to bring him down to earth for activities, but Ms. Starr said she didn't want him to be weighed down during foot painting.

"Don't worry about the product," she instructed. "Focus on the process. *Enjoy* the process!"

Nory didn't mind most of Ms. Starr's UDM activities. She found interpretive dance super awkward—all that flailing about and pretending to *be* the song—and she knew Bax hated headstands, but a lot of their exercises seemed to be working. Since she'd started at Dunwiddle Magic School, Nory had learned to control her magic more often. She could now hold a kitten shape long enough to go to after-school kittenball class. She'd also gotten better at making mixed animals, like the dritten, the way she wanted to, and at keeping hold of her human mind.

Nory liked the feel of paint on her feet. She chose purple and walked the length of the long sheet of paper and back, stepping just along one edge. Pepper painted each of her toes a different color and then pressed them neatly into the paper. Marigold and

Sebastian were trying to paint with just their heels, sitting on the floor. Bax had made a detailed picture of a castle with his toes.

Andres had small paper cups of paint lined up on top of the ladder, but he kept accidentally tipping them over onto people. "Sorry!" he cried as bright red paint splashed down. "Sorry again!" he called as Nory's hair got doused with yellow.

Nory was reaching for a paper towel when the bell rang.

"Oh, dear," Ms. Starr called out. "I forgot we have an assembly today! Right now, in fact! I'm sorry." She took in her students' paint-covered bodies. Marigold was wiping off her hearing aid. Bax had huge handprints on his shirt. Everyone had wet, paint-covered feet. Ms. Starr herself still had shoes on, but her jeans and hot-pink cardigan were spattered with paint from Andres's accidents. Her dark brown skin and neat, braided bun had splashes of white all over them. "No time for cleaning up. We'll just go as we are!" She shooed everyone up and out of the room. "To the auditorium, everyone!"

"This is so awkward," said Pepper. "How can we expect people to stop calling us wonkos when we show up at an assembly *looking* like wonkos?"

"On the bright side," Nory answered, "we get to track footprints *in the hall*!" She turned to watch the mess they were making as they walked.

"I feel bad for the janitor," said Pepper.

Outside the auditorium, the UDM class lined up next to the fifth-grade Flares.

Drat.

Being next to the Flares meant being next to the Sparkies, a group of snooty Flares led by Lacey Clench. Lacey was enormously mean and extremely committed. It was a dangerous combination.

All the Sparkies hated the UDM kids, in part because Lacey told them to. Lacey hated the way Nory and her classmates didn't fit any of the usual rules about magic. Also, Marigold had once shrunk Lacey to the size of a gerbil and Nory had once doused Lacey with skunkephant spray. The Sparkies had even tried unsuccessfully to kick the UDM kids out of Dunwiddle Magic School.

Now Lacey looked Nory up and down and pretended shock. She took off her large, round glasses and wiped them clean on the edge of her perfectly pressed blue cardigan. She tucked her short, sharply cut blond hair behind her ears and put the glasses back on.

"Zinnia, I think I'm seeing things," she said to her best friend, a girl with freckled pale skin and softly puffy red hair. "Are the wonkos changing colors?"

"We were painting, Lacey," Nory explained.

"I think they were painting," said Zinnia mildly.

"Don't be stupid, Zinnia," said Lacey. "They've all caught some wonky disease from each other and now they're melting like crayons, messing up the hallways. As if they haven't done enough damage already."

Her words stung, but Nory wouldn't let Lacey know that. "Oh, *I* see," she replied. "You're trying to make a joke. But you're not funny. Better luck next time."

"You're the ones who need luck," Lacey said. "Seeing you guys in the Show Off is going to be the best joke of all."

"The what?"

Lacey gave Nory a knowing, pitying look. "The Show Off. If you were even a little bit normal, you'd know what that is." Then her line started moving and she swished into the auditorium. Zinnia followed.

"What's the Show Off?" Nory asked Pepper as they slid into their seats.

Pepper shrugged.

Coach Vitomin stood behind the podium at the front of the auditorium. Not only was he Nory's fluxing tutor, he was also the head of the Fluxing Department and the coach of the kittenball team. He had big muscles.

"Arrrrre yoooooouuuu exxxx*cited*?!" Coach called out.

"Yeah!" almost everyone yelled.

Coach bounced along the stage. "The Show Off is a week from this Saturday! Here are the rules! Every class in every grade is invited to put together an act that shows off your talents! There will be one winning class per grade, plus some fun categories like Most Original, Most Hilarious, and Most Athletic. The competition will be intense. Intense, but fun!"

"I don't like this," Pepper whispered, tugging on Nory's sleeve. "I don't like this *at all*."

Coach went on. "Not every student has to participate, but for the love of vegetables, it's important to show school spirit. Your act can be anything so long as it's student work. Teachers aren't allowed to help. They *can* give you practice time during the school day, if lessons are done, but the Show Off performance is just like homework: Students have to do it on their own! Find extra time to work on your acts during recess or after school. Got it, everyone?" Coach asked.

"Got it!" most everyone yelled.

"And now, I give you . . ." Coach paused for effect.

"Last year's seventh-grade champs, and winners of Most Original and Most Athletic, the Flyers!"

Two drummers took seats at the edge of the stage and began a complicated rhythm. The Flyers, now eighth graders, walked out in formation. They wore silver T-shirts and held flashlights.

With a flick of a switch, the auditorium went dark. The Flyers started zooming across the room, over people's heads! Flashlights on, they made stars with their bodies. A sun. A comet. It was like a live star show at a planetarium, but grander. The Flyers came together and flew apart, everyone perfectly synchronized. The audience oohed and aahed. In the grand finale, the Flyers formed a giant *D* on the ceiling, for *Dunwiddle*.

The crowd roared their approval, stomping and clapping like mad.

"The Show Off is going to be *great*!" Nory cried.

"No," Pepper whispered. "The Show Off is going to be a nightmare."

4

Pepper's dad was a typical Fuzzy. Animals loved him, especially cats and dogs. He could get the grumpiest German shepherd to wag its tail. The neighborhood cats trotted up to him in the morning as he walked to work, offering him dead mice and snakes as gifts. Once, he'd even made a pit bull purr.

Pepper was the oldest Phan child. Her whole family had looked forward to her magic bubbling up around her tenth birthday—not just her parents, but also five-year-old Taffy and the three-year-old twins, Jam and Graham.

Sadly, the reaction of the Phans' beloved golden retriever, Toothpaste, was the first sign that something unusual had happened when Pepper's powers came in. When Pepper had greeted Toothpaste on her birthday morning, he'd trembled and peed on the floor. He'd let out a moan. His glossy yellow coat had turned stark white. He'd hurled himself at the front door, over and over, trying to get away from Pepper the Fierce. He'd actually hurt his shoulder doing it.

Pepper's family was horrified. Pepper was horrified, too—and heartbroken.

Mr. Phan's business, Furry Friends, brought dogs and cats to old people who needed company but couldn't take care of a pet any longer. Most of them lived in nursing homes or retirement communities. Many were stuck in wheelchairs or hospital beds. Mr. Phan brought the comfort animals to visit. The creatures were all thrilled to spend the day with him and would do anything he asked. He and his animal friends made people smile, every day.

Toothpaste had remained white, but his shoulder had healed after Mr. Phan took him to the vet. He couldn't come home again, though. He was too frightened of Pepper. He went to live at Furry Friends, which had a pleasant building and a big backyard for the animals to play in. Toothpaste was happy there and got along with the other comfort dogs.

But Pepper still missed him.

Today, Pepper's dad had picked up her sister from ordinary school and her brothers from nursery school. They were all in the kitchen when Pepper got home, but Pepper went straight up to her room and laid facedown on her bed.

She'd hated today's assembly about the stupid Show Off. She couldn't be in the same room with anyone who'd fluxed into an animal, or with any regular animals. She wouldn't be able to watch the Fluxer or the Fuzzy competition entries. And what "talent" was she supposed to show off, exactly? She couldn't be part of any act.

"Pep-Pep? Can we do the clappy thing?" It was her sister, Taffy.

"I'm not in the mood for the clappy thing," Pepper mumbled into her mattress.

"Would you take me to the playground, then? Please? Daddy said I can't play with the spray cleaner anymore."

"Okay," Pepper said. She could use some fresh air.

The playground was just a couple of blocks away. It had swings and a big sandbox, a climbing structure shaped like a fire engine, and a statue in the shape of a dragon. Pepper pushed Taffy on the swings.

"Pep-Pep, look!" Taffy cried, jamming her legs onto the ground to stop the swing. She pointed to a pair of redheaded girls, one in the sandbox and the other on the top of the climbing structure.

Pepper's stomach dropped. The older girl was Zinnia. Lacey's sidekick.

Taffy jumped off the swing. She tugged on Pepper's arm. "You have to help. You have to help!"

Pepper looked. Zinnia's little sister was running out of the sandbox at top speed. Behind her was a swarm of angry wasps.

She was screaming. The wasps were chasing her!

"Violet!" Zinnia cried out, seeing the wasps at the same time Pepper did.

Pepper charged over, flung her arms wide, and called on her fiercing magic on purpose, something she had done only one other time in her life.

"*Go!*" she thundered, feeling slippery all over.

The wasps froze midair. They hung in place for an impossible moment, then zoomed away in a fretful, buzzing line.

Just like that, they were gone.

Wow.

Wow!

Pepper was proud. And embarrassed. And tired. The good kind of tired, the way you feel after you've been swimming for a long time.

Violet flung herself at Zinnia and burst into tears. Pepper and Taffy hovered a few feet away.

"Thank you," Zinnia said to Pepper. Her cheeks were red. "Seriously, *thank* you. You saved her." She did a double take, and her expression changed. "Oh, it's you. Pepper."

"Yup," Pepper said, bracing herself for whatever cruelty came next.

"You saved my sister." Zinnia looked Pepper in the eye gratefully. "You didn't have to do that."

"Those wasps were dangerous."

"I couldn't think of anything to do," said Zinnia. She fluttered her hands. "I can't make a firebomb or anything flaming out of thin air."

"I got stung by a wasp," Violet whimpered, showing her wrist, which had a red welt on it. "Can we get ice cream? With Taffy?"

"You two know each other?" Pepper asked her sister.

Taffy nodded. "Not that good yet. She's in Mr. Grapefruit's class."

Violet tugged on Zinnia's arm. "I need ice cream to calm down." She swept her arm to indicate Pepper and Taffy, her gesture so grand that Pepper had to fight back a laugh. "We *all* need ice cream. I know you have money, Zinnia. You should treat our friends to say thank you for what Taffy's sister did."

"Oh." Pepper was flustered. It was one thing to save Zinnia's sister from a swarm of wasps. It was another thing entirely to eat ice cream with Zinnia in a place where other people could see them.

"Please say yes. It's my treat," Zinnia pleaded.

How can I say no? Pepper thought. *I can't say no.* So she didn't.

5

Nory woke up and twirled across her bedroom the next morning. She put on her red jeans, her red sneakers, and her white shirt with cherries on it. She bounced out of her bedroom and poured a bowl of Fruity Doodles. She was alone in the house. Aunt Margo was a Flyer who ran a one-woman airborne taxi service, so she left early for work some mornings.

Nory didn't bother with milk. She ate the Fruity Doodles straight. Then she put her hair in a high

ponytail and brushed her teeth because she'd promised Aunt Margo she would.

She felt lucky, wearing what she wanted to wear
and eating what she wanted to eat. Father had insisted
on protein like eggs or sausage every morning, and he
never allowed sugary cereal. Also, he liked Nory to
wear a dress and have her hair tightly braided.
Mornings with her brother, Hawthorn, and her sister, Dalia, had been busy, busy, busy: Father wiped
counters and Nory took out the trash; Hawthorn
cooked; Dalia's bunnies hopped about and got in the
way while she cleared the table. People finished up
homework and Father made phone calls and no one
stopped moving until they left the house for school
and work.

Nory didn't miss that at all.

Okay, maybe she missed it a little bit.

But she liked it here at Aunt Margo's, too. She
opened the door to a glorious day. The sky was a
shimmering blue. The sun was an egg yolk. Not
a rain cloud in sight.

She stepped out—and tripped on a box.

It was a brown package addressed to Nory Horace. No return address.

How odd.

Nory knelt and opened the box. *Ooh,* it was a present! Inside the brown paper mailer was a shiny purple box with a white ribbon. She opened the box and pulled out a pair of size four purple rain boots. Stripy purple rain boots! Nory's heart did a happy flip.

She loved them. She loved them *sooo* much.

She kicked off her sneakers and tugged them on. A perfect fit! A perfect present.

But who had sent it? Had Aunt Margo ordered them for Nory?

Nory ran back inside and grabbed an umbrella. Now she was hoping for rain.

Maybe Willa could help her out.

At school, morning meeting was dedicated to a discussion of the Show Off. "Let's start by sharing our hopes and fears about the event," Ms. Starr said. "Don't make a plan for an act just yet. Let's first express our feelings."

"I don't have any feelings," said Bax.

"I have a feeling of dread," said Pepper.

"I have a feeling of dread, too," said Marigold, her pencil shrinking in her hand as she spoke.

"I have a lot of emotions swirling inside of me," said Sebastian. "Zoom. Whoosh. Bang." Most people would have said these words loudly, but Sebastian kept them quiet, because he could see sound waves. He was an Upside-Down Flicker. Loud noises bothered him, because he could *see* them.

"We don't have to do an act at all," Bax said. "It's optional."

"Every class always does one," said Andres, from over their heads. He knew this stuff because of his older sister, Carmen. "Not every kid is in the act, but the only time a class didn't offer one was the year the sixth-grade Flickers all gave one another lice. So I think we should. My emotion is eagerness."

"I want to do it!" Nory said. "My emotion is excitement."

Bax groaned. "That's because you have cool magic, Nory."

"I have *embarrassing* magic," said Nory, sharply. "But I think we could figure something out that nobody else in the whole school could do. We might actually win the fifth grade."

Elliott nodded. "I'm feeling like I agree with Nory."

Willa nodded, too. "I'm feeling like I agree with Elliott, who agrees with Nory."

"That's because you and Elliott did the snowball prank," said Bax. "Rain magic and ice magic—those are cool talents. I'm feeling like you should think about the rest of us. The rest of us don't want to get laughed at by everyone at Dunwiddle."

"Are we having a vote?" Nory asked Ms. Starr. "I think half of us wants to and the other half doesn't."

"We're not having a vote," said Ms. Starr. "The truth is, UDM is going to enter the Show Off. Principal Gonzalez and Coach both told me they think we should. Our class really needs to connect with the larger Dunwiddle community."

Bax groaned.

Andres clapped.

Nory grinned.

When lunch rolled around, Nory herded the UDM kids to their usual table.

"Does anyone have any ideas for acts?" she asked.

Everyone stared at her blankly.

"No worries," Nory said. "Because I have one! I think Willa should make it rain! We could dance about with colorful umbrellas! And rain boots! Did you see my new rain boots?"

"Yes, Nory," Marigold said. "We all saw your mysterious new rain boots."

"Aren't they pretty?"

"So pretty," Pepper said.

"No dancing," said Bax.

"If Willa makes it rain, I could freeze the water,"

Elliott offered. "Maybe we could do an ice rink on the stage?"

"If Willa makes it rain, the audience might get soaked. Also, I can't skate," Sebastian said. "And I hate the ugly shriek of blades on ice." He shuddered.

"I can't skate, either," said Marigold.

"So: no dancing and no skating," said Willa.

"What about shrinking?" Elliott said. "Marigold could shrink something."

"Definitely no shrinking," Marigold said. "I don't know how to unshrink yet! Let Bax turn into a rock."

"No rock!" Bax put his head in his hands. "I am not getting wheelbarrowed to the nurse in front of the entire school."

Nory patted him. She knew he was sensitive. "We wouldn't wheelbarrow you until the curtain came down," she said.

"No rock," he said. "No way." Bax *was* making progress with his magic. Since tutoring with Coach, he could keep his human mind when he was in rock form, and he changed less often by accident. But being able to hear what people said about you when you turned into a helpless rock was actually pretty horrible.

Andres called down from the ceiling, where he was eating a ham sandwich. "I think we can't do snow or ice again," he said. "Everyone's seen the snow already with the snowball prank. We'll never win if that's what we do."

He had a point.

But what else could the UDM kids do that wouldn't go wonky?

6

Pepper waited for Ms. Starr in the Dunwiddle supply closet. It was a small room, but bigger than most closets. It was filled with mops and brooms, extra fire extinguishers, and bags of cat litter. You could sit on cardboard boxes. Pepper and Nory considered the supply closet their hideout. It was safe in there.

Today, Pepper had asked Ms. Starr if they could do their tutoring session in the closet, while the other UDM kids were at gym. Pepper thought it would make tutoring feel different from just staying in the

UDM classroom. Maybe something different would happen and they would make progress with her magic.

Ms. Starr had said yes: "Let's change it up a little! I agree."

Now Pepper waited for Ms. Starr while eating lemon drops from the small box she kept in her pocket. Finally, the doorknob twisted and Ms. Starr bustled in. "Ooh, it *is* kind of fun in here," she said, looking around. "I can see why you like it. I'm sorry I don't have an office where we can meet. First-year teachers rarely get them." She held a large box in her arms. "Guess what I brought today," she said, her eyes shining. She sat down on the floor and opened the box. Inside was the cutest rabbit Pepper had ever seen. "She's a fawn Miniature Cashmere Lop," Ms. Starr said. "Her name is Carrot."

Pepper leaned in. Carrot had long, floppy ears that fell straight down below her round face. Her body was also round. Her brown eyes were bright and curious, and her orangey-brown fur was as fluffy as a dandelion in bloom, the kind you made a wish on.

"Hi, Carrot," Pepper said, so entranced by the puffball in front of her that she forgot to worry about frightening it.

"Greetings," Carrot replied.

It talked!

Zamboozle!

Pepper flew backward, shocked. Her head banged a shelf loaded with bars of soap. A dozen of them showered down on her.

"Are you all right?" Carrot asked. "I didn't mean to scare you."

Pepper nodded. She was too amazed to speak.

Carrot put her paws on the edge of the box, standing on her hind legs. "My uncle Alphonse got hit on the head by a bar of soap. After that he was cross-eyed and ate nothing but apple slices for the rest of his life. I hope that doesn't happen to you."

"I'm fine, really," said Pepper. "My eyes aren't crossed, are they?"

She leaned forward and Carrot mirrored her actions, sniffing.

"They look all right to me," the rabbit said.

Pepper swallowed. "You're not afraid of me, are you?"

"Of *you*?" Carrot said. "No. Any student of Eloise's is a friend of mine. And you smell delightfully of citrus." She wiggled her nose. "Might I have it, perhaps? The lemony lozenge in your mouth?"

Since when do rabbits talk? Pepper thought. *And did she just call a lemon drop a lozenge? Also, I guess Ms. Starr's first name is Eloise. Huh!*

"Carrot's fairly unique," Ms. Starr said.

"Fairly?" Carrot shook her head and turned to Pepper. "Lozenge, please. My dignity is wounded. I need soothing."

Pepper opened the box of lemon drops and gave Carrot a fresh one. The rabbit snuffled it up. Her mouth tickled Pepper's palm.

"I've been searching for a companion animal like Carrot for a couple of months," Ms. Starr continued.

"She's a *very* special, definitely unique creature who can help you with your magic."

"Because she talks," Pepper filled in.

Ms. Starr laughed. "No. *All* rabbits talk."

"They do?" Pepper thought back on the rabbits she'd known through her dad's business, Furry Friends. Those rabbits had chirped and made snuffling sounds, but they hadn't *talked*.

"Not just rabbits," Ms. Starr explained. "Most animals talk. And certain Fuzzies can understand their language, though not all of them can."

Pepper frowned. "But Carrot's speaking English. Isn't she?"

"Yes. That's *my* Upside-Down Fuzzy magic. I enable animals to speak our language."

"Really?" Pepper asked. "Wow."

"It wasn't easy when I was young," Ms. Starr said. "When I was a girl in Fuzzy classes at school, no one had heard of upside-down magic. I had trouble turning my magic off and on. Animals near me would start complaining, arguing, or making inappropriate remarks, often in the middle of a teacher's lecture. I got in trouble a lot. And animals don't like me automatically, the way they like typical Fuzzies. So sometimes the things they'd say were very rude indeed. Especially basset hounds. You wouldn't believe what words some of them know. I have no idea how they learn that kind of vocabulary."

"You had trouble with your magic in school?" asked Pepper.

"Of course I did," said Ms. Starr. "I couldn't do lots of the regular beginner Fuzzy skills, like feeding unicorns. And my talent was very disruptive in a room full of animals. My parents were always supportive, but it wasn't until high school that I found a teacher who didn't think I should be ashamed of my upside-down magic. I learned so much from her that I decided to become a teacher myself."

"Wow," said Pepper again. Ms. Starr really *did* understand her UDM students. "But if all animals can speak your language when you magic them," she asked, "then what's special about Carrot?

You said you'd been looking for a pet like her for months."

"I prefer the term 'companion,'" Carrot said.

"Sorry," said Pepper. And then she opened her eyes wide. "Oh, I get it now. What's special about Carrot is that she's not afraid of me!"

Ms. Starr nodded. "Carrot is an extraordinary bunny. She is afraid of almost nothing, and she won Best in Show at the American Rabbit Breeders' Annual Competition."

"Can I pet her?" Pepper asked Ms. Starr.

Carrot cleared her throat.

"Oh. Sorry. Um, can I pet you?" Pepper asked Carrot.

The rabbit dipped her head in a bow. "You may."

Pepper wiped her sweaty palms on her jeans.

"It'll be okay," Ms. Starr said softly. "She's prepared for you."

Pepper nodded. She reached out her arm and laid her hand gently on Carrot's head. "You're so soft," she marveled.

"Cashmere," Carrot said modestly. She turned to Ms. Starr. "I can feel the magic coming from her, and it's definitely stronger when she touches me. But it's not that scary. It's more of an unpleasant tingle."

Pepper took her hand off Carrot.

"It's like a bug bite," the rabbit said. "No big deal. Really, those other animals should get it together."

Pepper patted the rabbit again. "Yesterday I scared off a swarm of wasps," she told Ms. Starr. "They were chasing a little girl in the park. I stopped them from stinging her."

"That's great," Ms. Starr said. "You know, your magic isn't a curse. Over time, you're going to find ways to help people with it. I really believe that."

Slowly, Pepper nodded. She really wanted to believe it, too.

That afternoon, Pepper took Taffy to the playground again. She didn't wait for Taffy to ask. She volunteered.

As they walked along the sidewalk, Taffy asked, "Can we play with Violet and Zinny?"

"Zinnia," Pepper corrected.

"Like the *Biscuits BeBop* character?"

"Yes." *Biscuits BeBop* was an animated TV show featuring a raccoon ballerina named Zinnia.

"Is Zinnia named after *Biscuits BeBop*?"

"No. At least, I don't think so."

"There they are!" Taffy cried. She waved both hands above her head. "Violet!"

Taffy and Violet squealed and dashed off to the swings. Pepper stepped hesitantly toward Zinnia. "Hi again."

"Hi."

Then they didn't know what to say.

"Taffy's convinced you're named after a *Biscuits BeBop* character," Pepper finally mumbled.

Zinnia smiled. "Nah. Just the flower. But I used to be really into *Biscuits BeBop*. When I was little."

"I remember that," Pepper said. She had gone to

ordinary school with Zinnia, Lacey, and a number of the UDM kids, although she hadn't been friends with them then. She had mostly kept to herself.

"You remember?" Zinnia raised her eyebrows.

"I was into it, too."

"Actually, I still like *Biscuits BeBop*." Zinnia lifted her chin. "Go on and make me feel stupid, if you're going to."

"Why would I make you feel stupid?" asked Pepper. "*Biscuits BeBop* will be cool forever."

Zinnia rubbed her forehead. "Sorry. Lacey makes fun of me a lot. I took my *BeBop* posters down when she wouldn't stop bugging me about them. I got rid of my *BeBop* backpack, too. But my mom says I should just tell the truth, so I was kind of trying that idea out on you."

"My friends tease me sometimes," said Pepper. "But they never make me feel stupid."

"Lacey is very, very good at making people feel stupid," Zinnia said.

Pepper bit her lower lip. Should she mention Lacey was a horrible, mean person and that sometimes Zinnia was, too? Or was Zinnia's confession a trap, to get Pepper to say something mean that Zinnia would go tell Lacey?

Pepper decided to try the truth. "Yeah, she's extremely good at making people feel stupid."

"This whole year, she's gotten meaner and meaner," Zinnia confessed. "Which I know you know, because she's been so awful to you guys."

Pepper scrunched her toes in her sneakers.

"She's not *all* bad," Zinnia quickly added. "I've lived next door to her my whole life, and she has a ton of cool ideas. In second grade, we dug this enormous hole in her backyard that was big enough to call a cave. We used to go in there and have picnics and play with dolls. It was all her idea. She got the shovels and everything. And we had bike races in the vacant lot down on Cherry Blossom Road. Lacey organized all these kids from our block. But then she applied to some fancy private magic academy for fifth grade, and she didn't get in. Her parents were very disappointed in her. I think they made her feel bad. Ever since, she's been trying to make everyone else feel bad. At least, that's what it seems like to me." Abruptly, Zinnia stopped talking. She stared hard at the ground. "Could you please not tell anyone I told you that? Lacey would kill me if she knew. I try to stay on her good side."

"Why?"

"Well, you've seen how she treats the people on her bad side."

Pepper got it. "I won't tell. I promise."

Zinnia blinked several times in a row. "I'm sorry about how I acted when Lacey made that petition to get rid of your class, though," she said. "And about the flaming tennis balls and the mean stuff we said about the UDM kids. I shouldn't have gone along with all that. I feel really bad."

Pepper didn't know how to respond. She didn't

want to say it was okay, what Zinnia and the other Sparkies had done, because it wasn't. But she didn't want to refuse the apology, either. "My parents named me after a spice," she blurted.

Zinnia lifted her head.

"'Please pass the pepper,' big kids used to say," Pepper continued. "And then they would! They'd pick me up and pass me around the playground!"

"That's awful!"

"Or they'd have sneezing fits and say, 'It's Pepper! I'm allergic to Pepper!'"

Zinnia half smiled. "When I was in kindergarten, two girls tried to *plant* me."

"When I was in kindergarten, two boys tried to *sprinkle* me! Over their lunches!"

"Zamboozle," Zinnia said, shaking her head.

"Zamboozle," Pepper agreed.

They got on the swings and pumped their legs. They zoomed higher than airplanes, while Taffy and Violet played dump trucks in the sandbox.

They stayed in the playground until the sun started to set. The sky turned blue and orange, and Pepper said it looked like mixed-berry ice cream.

"It totally does," Zinnia said. She cocked her head to the side. "I kind of want to eat it."

Pepper laughed. She stuck out her tongue and pretended to lick the air and said, "Delicious."

7

It was Tuesday Night Tigerball on TV. Nory, Aunt Margo, and Aunt Margo's boyfriend, Figs, ate dinner in front of the screen. Figs was a Fluxer, too, but he only did dogs. His favorite shape was a big, slobbery Saint Bernard.

Tigerball was played by Fluxers in tiger form. Tonight it was the Burlington Bengals swatting against the Mandalay Saber-Tooths. The Bengals had the lead. They were going to win. Bengals all the way!

Nory was hoping to get on the school kittenball

team in seventh grade. Kittenball was what you played until you got licensed for a tiger.

When the game had been on about an hour, the phone rang in the kitchen. Nory hopped up to answer it. "Hello?"

"Nory!" two voices chorused.

"Hawthorn?" Nory imagined her older brother, age sixteen, with his short crinkly hair and always-clean sports jersey. Huddled beside him would be her sister, age thirteen, no doubt with a bat or a bunny perched on her shoulder. "Dalia?"

A flood of words made Nory's head spin:

"We miss you!"

"Hawthorn's entered the hot wax art competition at Father's school, Sage Academy, but I don't think he has a chance."

"Dalia got a fish tank for her birthday with squid in it."

"How's Aunt Margo?"

"Is she still letting you eat Fruity Doodles?"

"We didn't tell Father about the Fruity Doodles."

"We got the invite your school sent us."

"But what's a 'Show Off'?"

"Will you be in the performance? Are you going to do something wonky?"

Nory hadn't known families would be invited to the Show Off. Then again, at Sage Academy, where Dalia and Hawthorn went, parents and relatives were always being invited to spell-a-thons, fly races, and invisible diving competitions.

"I'm sure she's learned a lot at her new school," Hawthorn said to Dalia. "She's not going to wonk out onstage."

Nory gripped the phone. In the living room, she heard Aunt Margo yell. The Bengals must have scored. Part of her wanted to get back to the game, but Hawthorn and Dalia were her brother and sister. She loved them.

"We want to come and see you."

Nory's stomach suddenly felt much fuller than it

had before. She leaned against the kitchen counter. "Did Father say you could come to the show?" she asked weakly.

Hawthorn and Dalia fell silent. Nory could practically see them giving each other meaningful looks.

"He didn't exactly say that," Hawthorn confessed. "But he didn't say no, either."

"I'm going to nag him," Dalia pronounced. "And then when Father sees you being a regular Fluxer, he'll be so proud."

Nory's legs trembled. She *wasn't* learning to be a regular Fluxer. She was learning to expand the possibilities of her Upside-Down Magic. She'd been practicing her dritten with Coach, just that afternoon. "Urmp," she said.

"Dalia, you're stressing Nory out," Hawthorn said.

Somewhere in the distance, in the halls of the ritzy, echoey house her brother and sister were calling from, Nory heard the sound of a door. She heard the jangle of keys and the authoritative thump of footsteps. *Father.*

"Ah, hey, we should go," Hawthorn said.

"We should let you get back to whatever you were doing," Dalia added. "But, real quick, did you get the boots?"

"What boots?"

"The rain boots! Aunt Margo told Father you needed rain boots, and so Father—"

"The boots are from *Father*? I love those boots!"

No way.

Father had given her a present? A good present?

For real?

"Well, *I* picked them out," Dalia said. "He wouldn't know you like purple. But he said I could, and he paid for them and boxed them and took them to the post office."

"He's always believed in proper footwear," said Hawthorn.

Nory heard Father's deep voice say something about dinner.

"Oh, zwingo, we've got to go," Dalia said.

"We'll call again when we can," Hawthorn promised. "Just don't go wonky at the Show Off! We'll get Father there and everything will be great."

There was a click. The line went dead.

Zamboozle. Father was coming to the Show Off? They were all coming? Nory felt woozy.

"Nory?" Aunt Margo called from in front of the television. "Are you coming back?"

"Of course!" she said brightly. But what Nory really wanted to do was turn into a beaver-kitten, build a bitten lodge in the backyard, and hide in it until after the Show Off was done.

8

P epper met Ms. Starr at Dunwiddle early the next morning for extra tutoring time. She was already there when the teacher arrived at the supply closet with Carrot in the box. "She's not in a box at home," the teacher explained as she sat down. "At home she's got free run of the yard and there's a little rabbit door that leads inside."

Carrot hopped out and climbed into Pepper's lap. She wiggled importantly. "I can feel the buzz of your magic, Pepper," the rabbit said, "but it's just an annoyance. I can take it. In fact, today we thought you could *try* to scare me. Go on." She paused. And waited. "Are you trying yet?"

"No," Pepper confessed. "I don't *want* to scare you."

"Do you *want* to get the hang of your magic?" asked Carrot. "Because Eloise *said* you wanted to get the hang of your magic! She and I went over a whole lesson plan."

Ms. Starr nodded.

"Then scare me," Carrot demanded. She held her pink nose high in the air and adopted a brave countenance, as if preparing to be given a shot.

"Um . . . boo," Pepper said.

Carrot bolted out of Pepper's lap, as if electrocuted. Her fur stood on end and her ears stood straight up. She shrieked as if she were being murdered.

Pepper cringed. Oh, no! Had she given poor Carrot a heart attack?

"Carrot!" Ms. Starr cried, scooping the bunny into her arms. "Are you all right?"

Abruptly, Carrot stopped shrieking and thrashing. She straightened her whiskers with her paw. She shook her fluffy tail.

"I was kidding!" the rabbit chided. She eyed Pepper. "You didn't *really* think you'd scared me, did you?"

"That was a trick?" Pepper said. "You looked like you were being electrocuted!"

"Rabbits have a lot of dramatic flair. Half of that nose twitching you see common garden rabbits do is for show, don't you know?" Carrot cocked her ears. "This time, don't insult me by saying 'Boo.'"

"What she means is, try to feel the magic inside you, Pepper," said Ms. Starr. "Remember the way we talked about feeling the paint in the foot-painting exercises. It feels ticklish, and you can use it creatively. Right? You can decide what you want to do with it. You know how it felt when we painted. Now see if you can feel it with your magic."

Pepper felt inside herself.

She *could* feel the magic.

She hadn't ever really been able to understand what part of her was magic and what part of her was just Pepper. But now she could.

She focused on Carrot. Then she imagined that she was an electric fence, and that her magic was the electricity. *Go! Go!* She imagined crackling bolts of energy, the way she had with the wasps. *Go!*

This time, Carrot didn't fluff herself up or stiffen her ears or squeal. Silently, she dove headfirst behind the boxes of cat litter.

Pepper let her magic relax. She stood up and peeked over into the very narrow crack between the boxes of litter and the wall. The bunny was squashed in there, shaking.

Hiding!

Ms. Starr bent over and touched Carrot's back. "You all right, my friend?"

"Mrwwfflfel," said Carrot.

"What?"

"Monster magic!" said Carrot a little louder.

"Are you ready to come out?" asked Ms. Starr gently.

Carrot wiggled backward until she was out of the crack. When she was back in the center of the supply room floor, she shook herself like a dog. "Wow," she said finally. "I didn't really think you could scare me."

"I'm sorry," said Pepper.

"It's okay! I asked you to. Eloise is rewarding me with a huge broccoli for helping you, so don't worry. I'm getting paid! Wow, again. It was like you turned into a horrible monster. Congratulations! You are a very strong magician when you put your mind to it."

That didn't make Pepper feel better. "I don't want to be a horrible monster."

"Don't be so dramatic," Carrot said. "What you do with your magic is under your control. Or it *will* be. Hopefully. *You're* not a horrible monster. You just *can be* one—if you have to be. And that's very cool. I really have to respect you, Pepper."

Carrot climbed into her lap, which made Pepper feel a little better. But there was still a lot she didn't understand.

At lunch, Pepper got pasta, cauliflower casserole, and apple slices. She went to sit with the UDM kids, as usual.

Nory was already sitting down. She had dark circles under her eyes, and she hunched over her food, stabbing her casserole but never taking a bite.

"Nory? Are you okay?" Pepper asked.

"Huh?" Nory blinked.

Elliott sat down beside Pepper, making the table jump when he banged down his tray. "Listen up, people," he said. "Every other fifth-grade class knows what they're doing for the Show Off. Every class but us. We have to nail down a plan."

"How do *you* know *they* know?" Marigold asked, sitting on Pepper's other side. She parked Andres on his leash above them.

"Bax heard it from Nurse Riley," said Elliott. "Nurse Riley knows all the gossip. Kids open up to him while they're getting ice packs or having frogs taken out of their noses." Bax himself was still at the back of the lunch line with Sebastian. As Willa sat down, Elliott counted off on his fingers: "Nurse Riley told Bax that the Fuzzies are commanding a camel. The Fluxers are doing a kitten dance. The Flickers are doing something called Oranges Away! The Flyers are doing a traditional flag dance, and the Flares have some sort of colored-light-firefly thing. We need to come up with something good. Right, Nory?"

Nory seemed to be in a daze. "What?"

"You wanted us to enter!" Elliott slapped the table. "So let's figure something out!"

"He's right," Marigold said. "We can moan and gripe, or we can come up with an idea."

"I vote for moaning and griping," Bax said, taking his seat.

Pepper figured now was her best chance to speak

up. "I'm not going to be in the Show Off," she told them. "I'm not even going to be in the audience, because I'll fierce the animals. Anyone who wants to opt out, we could go get ice cream that night or something."

"Ice cream?" said Bax. "Count me in."

"No, you guys, wait till you hear what I've been thinking!" Elliott said. "We could do a drama. Like, Nory could flux into a spider. Willa would stand on a chair and go, 'Oh, no! Oh, no! A spider!'"

Willa snorted. "Or not."

"Then Bax could walk onto the stage as himself, just a regular guy—but maybe with a mustache?"

"Why a mustache?" Andres called down.

"Dramatic effect," Elliott said, warming to his idea. "Bax could say, 'Oh, dear, I see you have spider problems. No need to fear, rock man is here!' And then Bax could turn into a rock and I could come on and roll him. Right before he squishes Nory to a pulp, KABOOM! He turns back into a boy!"

Elliott's face was alight. He looked at the other UDM kids.

They stared back.

"If anyone is going to get rid of a spider, it would be Pepper," Marigold said.

"I don't *need* to be saved from Spider-Nory!" Willa exclaimed. "What if I *like* spiders? My aunt Jen's a Fluxer and she always does spiders!"

"I don't even *do* spider yet," said Nory, shaking her head.

"And no one would see the spider from the stage," called Andres.

"I wouldn't be able to turn back," said Bax.

"Isn't that what you're working on in tutoring?" asked Elliott.

"A little," said Bax. "But I haven't actually done it yet. It's crazy tricky to flux back when you're an inanimate object. Coach has me working on other stuff, too."

Sebastian joined them. As was his custom during

lunch, he wore a large plastic cone around his head to block the sound waves from his vision in the cafeteria. "I heard there will be hundreds of people at the Show Off," he said. "If everyone's family comes."

Nory gulped. "H-hundreds? We can't do a spider drama with hundreds of people watching!"

"I'm trying to find an idea! If you guys don't like the spider story, come up with one yourself!" Elliot said, raising his voice.

"We just can't embarrass ourselves!" Nory said. "I mean . . . I don't know. This is a big deal. Bigger, maybe, than we first realized."

Nory worked her mouth as if she wanted to say more, then pushed back from the table and took off.

Pepper hurried after her. "Nory! Nory, wait up!" she called.

Pepper could tell Nory was upset about more than just finding an act for the Show Off. She ran into the hall, but it was empty.

Had Nory fluxed again, accidentally?

Maybe she'd gone to see Coach in his office, or maybe she'd headed to the bathroom.

Pepper walked down the hall toward the supply closet. That seemed to be the most likely hiding place. On the way, she passed the Flare lab. Inside, she could hear two girls arguing.

Pepper peeked in. It was Lacey and Zinnia. Lacey's features were screwed up like a rotten peach. Her skin was blotchy. Zinnia was on the verge of tears. "I'm not going to be in the Show Off!" she said. "I hate performing, and I'd rather just watch. I told you a million times. You can't make me!"

"I can so make you," Lacey said harshly, squeezing her fists by her sides. "I can so. Because I! Am! The Boss!"

"Not! Of! Me!" Zinnia cried. "Not anymore!"

Pepper backed away from the Flare lab door and hurried to the supply closet before either of them saw her. She slipped inside the closet and, sure enough, Nory was there. She was sitting in the dark with her head in her hands.

Pepper flipped on the light and offered Nory a cherry unicorn gummy from the bag in her pocket. "Unicorn?"

"Thanks."

"Have as many as you want. Are you okay?"

"I guess."

"What's wrong?" asked Pepper, sitting down.

Nory shrugged. "The Show Off."

"What about it?"

"Well, you know I don't live with my dad, right? Just with my aunt."

Pepper knew.

"Well," Nory explained, "Father sent me to Dunwiddle to go to UDM, but he also sent me *away* from our home in Nutmeg. Because my wonky magic upsets him. It's embarrassing, and it makes life crazy, and I was always destroying the furniture. I haven't even talked to him since I left. He hasn't called. Or written. Or visited. The only thing he did was send me rain boots, and that was great—it was nice he thought to send me a present—but it also made me care again. Like, I was able to pretend I didn't miss him until I got the rain boots. And then I missed him a lot. And they didn't have a note. And now he's coming to the Show Off."

"So you *can't* opt out of performing," said Pepper, putting the pieces together. "Because if you do, your dad won't visit."

Nory nodded. "But I also can't do anything wonky onstage, or he'll never visit again."

Poor Nory.

Pepper hated her magic, and she hated not having a dog anymore, but her parents were always proud of her. She loved that they were proud of her.

They sat in silence. They each ate another cherry unicorn gummy.

Finally Pepper said, "Guess what I heard just now when I went by the Flare lab? It's about Lacey Clench."

Nory brightened. "Ooh, is she plotting evil?"

"Not exactly," said Pepper. "She's *failing* to plot evil."

"We should get out the chocolate for this," said Nory, standing up to pull a bag of choco fire trucks from their secret hiding place. She sat back down with the bag and crossed her legs. "Okay. Tell me all about it."

9

That afternoon, Nory went with Bax to meet with their fluxing tutor, Coach Vitomin. Coach smelled like sweat and herbal tea. He made them both eat disgusting high-nutrient foods, like seaweed and sardines, which he said were important for fluxing. But Nory thought he was a good teacher.

Nory had been working on keeping her human mind when she was a dritten. Bax was working on turning into objects other than just rocks. He was making progress.

"Ready, Bax?" said Coach Vitomin. "Go!"

Bax scrunched up his face and then, suddenly, fluxed. His head wobbled on his shoulders, there were some popping sounds, and . . . he became a swivel chair. Not a rock, but a swivel chair.

"Zamboozle!" cried Nory.

"Fantastic. Are you still in touch with your human mind, son?" asked Coach Vitomin.

Swivel-Bax started to spin. Around and around and around.

"Amazing!" Nory said. Bax had never been able to move before. His rock couldn't roll. But this new swivel chair swiveled like crazy!

Swivel-Bax stopped, teetering from side to side.

"I think he made himself dizzy," Coach said.

"I didn't know a chair could look sick," said Nory.

"We know he probably can't turn back," said Coach. "We better take him to Riley. But good job, son. That was really something, there, with the swiveling."

Nory steered Swivel-Bax to Nurse Riley's office

for his medicine. At least she didn't have to use the wheelbarrow. In fact, Swivel-Bax could roll his own wheels. He just didn't seem to know which direction to roll them.

Nory had kittenball after school. After practice, she walked home with Elliott. He had stayed late for Flare tutoring.

"The Fluxers are definitely doing a dance to that song 'Kitty Grooves,'" Nory told Elliott as they walked. "Half are going to be butterscotch kittens. The other half are going to be black. They're going to be in pairs." She sighed. "They're doing back spins and leg breaks and nae naes."

"Whatever. We'll find something better." Elliott kicked a pebble.

"I hope. Guess what Pepper found out?"

"What?"

"The Sparkies are losing their spark. Zinnia and Lacey are fighting, and Zinnia might skip the Show Off."

"I highly doubt that."

"No, seriously. Pepper heard them."

"Okay, but, Nory? Zinnia's *always* done everything Lacey tells her to. Just like I used to do everything Lacey told *me*, back in ordinary school."

"Well, today Zinnia told Lacey that she wasn't the boss of her."

"I don't buy it. Remember, I hung out with those kids from kindergarten till fourth grade." Elliott widened his eyes, then nodded in a knowing way. "Never mind. Now I get it."

"Now you get what?"

"Just tell me this: Did they know Pepper was there?"

Nory frowned. "No. I don't think so. How would they? Pepper eavesdropped. But not on purpose."

Again, he nodded. "I think they knew. Nory, how many times have the Sparkies played tricks on us?"

"Too many times to count?"

"Exactly. They're up to something."

"But—"

"Nory, if Pepper saw Lacey and Zinnia fighting, it's because they wanted her to. They *planned* it. It was a performance."

Nory bit her lip.

"Don't believe me? Let's go talk to Pepper," Elliott said. He veered onto Magnolia Street, and Nory trailed behind. They passed the small neighborhood playground and took a left onto Spiderweb Street, where Pepper lived. Elliott marched right up to Pepper's cute blue house and rang the doorbell.

"She might not be home," Nory said, suddenly feeling nervous.

The door opened and Pepper grinned. "Elliott! Nory! Hi!"

One of her twin brothers clung to her leg. The other toddled behind her with two wooden spoons. Their hair stuck straight up on their heads and they had fat, round wrists. "Bam jam bam!" the second one yelled, beating the spoons together.

From within the house came a boom. It sounded like cymbals crashing together, but deeper.

"Pep-Pep, now!" Nory heard a little voice say. "'Crazy-Daisy Shame'!"

Pepper turned bright red. "Taffy! Shush!"

"But you promised!" Then another bang, then footsteps. A chubby-cheeked little girl in overalls and pigtails wiggled her way into the frame of the open front door. "Hi! Pep-Pep's taking care of us. It's the law. And she's going to do the clappy thing for 'Crazy-Daisy Shame,' aren't you, Pep-Pep?" She gave Nory and Elliott a no-nonsense look. "'Cause that's the law, too." She ushered Nory and Elliott inside with a flourish of her arm. "Come. You may be the audience."

Elliott grinned. He and Nory followed Taffy to a battered sofa surrounded by upturned mixing bowls of different sizes.

"The song 'Crazy-Daisy Shame'?" Nory asked Pepper. "By Everyday Cake?" Everyday Cake was one of Nory's favorite bands. Everyday Cake was one of *everybody's* favorite bands.

"No clappy thing with people here," Pepper told Taffy.

"I love Everyday Cake," Nory said. She was trying to be nice. She could see Pepper was anxious.

The twin who had been attached to Pepper's leg slid free and went to the biggest mixing bowl and sat behind it. The twin with the spoons went over, too. He smacked the spoons rhythmically, and his brother picked up the beat on the bowl, drumming his palms against the top.

"Wow," Nory said. She and Elliott had come to Pepper's house for a reason—hadn't they? She couldn't remember what it was now.

"I'll sing," Taffy said. She grabbed Pepper and pushed her front and center. "You do the clappy thing." Pepper's face was flushed and her eyes were wide. "I'll get your baby pictures if you don't!" Taffy threatened. "The ones where you're nakey-nakey!"

"Come on, Pepper," Elliott said. "I know how it goes. I'm going to love it no matter what."

"Me too," said Nory. Pepper had such a nice family. Nory could already tell that whatever they were going to do would be super fun.

Pepper smiled. "Okay, you guys," she said to Elliott and Nory. "This is just something we do after school some days, when I'm looking after them."

"Clappy thing!" Elliott chanted. "Clappy thing!"

And then . . . magic happened. Not *magic* magic, but music magic. Clapping magic.

Pepper's hands moved like birds all over her body, slapping, tapping, swish-swash thwapping. She did with her hands what the members of Everyday Cake did with keyboard, guitar, and electric violin. Right on cue, Taffy belted out the lyrics to their number-one hit "Crazy-Daisy Shame."

When the chorus came around again, Elliott joined in, and so did Nory.

Together, everyone brought home the chorus:

Don't don't don't
It's a crazy-daisy shame
Don't keep your honey bunch
Out in the rain

Open that door
I'll come in and get dry
Don't don't don't
Don't pass me by!

They yelled the last bit, just like the real band did. Taffy jumped up and down with delight. Elliott whooped, and Pepper laughed and covered her face.

"Wow, Pepper, that was awesome!" Nory cried.

Taffy cleared her throat purposefully.

"And you, too, Taffy! All of you were fantastic! But, Pepper, why didn't you tell us?"

"Tell you, what?" Pepper said. "That I know how to clap?"

"Pepper!" Nory said. "That was *not* clapping. That was . . . I don't even know what it was. Just, zamboozle!"

Elliott pointed at Pepper as if something had fallen into place. "You took percussion lessons with my dad! You were the girl he was always talking about, weren't you? You took lessons up until last summer, and then . . ."

Pepper and Elliott exchanged a look.

"Oh," Elliott said sheepishly.

"What?" Nory demanded.

"My magic came in," Pepper said. "And Elliott has three cats." Pepper twisted her fingers together. "So . . . I quit."

"My dad asked her to leave," Elliott told Nory bitterly. He turned to Pepper. "But I didn't know it was you. I swear. He said he had a problem with a student, and that was why Puffy and Cuddles and Mike were hiding under the sink yowling every week. I thought it was because some kid had been *mean* to them."

"He didn't *make* me quit," Pepper said. "He said it wasn't fair to the cats, because they weren't outdoor cats, so they couldn't get away. He said that once I got my fiercing under control, he'd be happy to have me back." She smiled ruefully. "I mean, he didn't call it *fiercing*. He didn't know what to call it! But it wasn't his fault, Elliott."

"Guys!" cried Nory. She had a good idea. "We should have a band!"

Elliott's eyes widened. "We should!"

"We won't have to use our upside-down magic at all! We'll just use our *musical* talents!"

"You want us to sing 'Crazy-Daisy Shame' for the Show Off?" Pepper said.

"Yes! Elliott plays guitar. Pepper, you'll do percussion. I can sing!"

Their faces fell, but Nory didn't have time to find out why, because the doorbell rang.

"I'll get it, I'll get it!" Taffy said, sprinting to the door.

Nory heard voices. Pepper headed after Taffy, and Nory followed curiously. Elliott came along as well.

"—I'm babysitting, as usual on Wednesday," a girl was saying. Her face was blocked by the door. "So do you and Taffy want to go to the park again? And your brothers, if you're looking after them, too."

"Oh," Pepper said. She glanced back down the hall at Nory, clearly flustered. "Well . . ."

Nory came forward, and when she saw who it was, her mouth fell open.

Zinnia Clarke was on the porch.

Zinnia!

Clarke!

Zinnia the Sparky! Zinnia the cruel! Zinnia who had signed the petition to get rid of UDM! Zinnia who had called all the UDM kids horrible names! Zinnia who had thrown fireballs at them! Zinnia who had taunted them and mocked them and who always did Lacey's evil bidding.

Nory sensed Elliott behind her.

"What are you doing here?" he asked Zinnia.

"Nothing," she said. "I just—"

"Leave Pepper alone," snapped Elliott. "I don't care if she scared your dog or upset your hamster.

She's doesn't fierce on purpose. And since I know you don't know what *nice* means, I'll put it in words you can understand: Pepper is on *our* team. So leave before I ice your socks."

Zinnia went pale. "Pepper," she said. "Please. Would you explain?"

"What's there to explain?" Elliott scoffed. "Nory still has a burn scar from the flaming tennis balls you threw at her. You helped melt my bike tires. You helped start the petition against us, and you let Lacey burn Andres's leash! You've been doing mean things ever since you got your powers."

"Tell them I'm your friend," Zinnia begged Pepper.

Elliott stepped toward Zinnia. "You are *not* her friend. *We're* her friends. So just leave her ALONE."

"I'm not that person anymore," Zinnia said.

"You're not Zinnia Clarke?" Elliott said. "Who are you, then?"

A spy, Nory thought. "She's a spy!" she blurted. "She's spying on UDM! Through Pepper! For the Show Off!"

"That's why you staged your pretend fight with Lacey, isn't it?" Elliott said as Zinnia stared at the floor. "I told you, Nory. I told you it was staged."

"I'm sorry, Pepper," Nory added. "But it's got to be true. Zinnia is a total faker."

Pepper's eyes were wide. Nory couldn't tell what she was thinking.

"I think all of you should leave," Pepper finally said in a soft voice. "Go home. I'm very busy babysitting."

10

Pepper pulled Nory aside first thing the next morning, before Nory made it up the steps to Dunwiddle's wide front entrance.

"Can I talk to you?" Pepper asked.

"You kicked us out of your house," Nory said.

"I was upset."

"It hurt my feelings."

"You hurt *my* feelings."

Nory's eyebrows flew up. "I did?"

Pepper pulled Nory away from the throng of

arriving students. "Well, you and Elliott. You guys were so mean to Zinnia. Like, really mean."

"Yeah," Nory said reluctantly. "But everything Elliott said was true. He was friends with all of them before. Lacey, Rune, Zinnia: They were his best buddies until everyone's magic came in. They were so mean about his freezing. Evil, even. That's how this whole trouble with the Sparkies started."

"Don't you think it was mostly Lacey who gave him a hard time, though?" Pepper said.

"She wasn't working alone," Nory pointed out. "Not ever."

"I told you Zinnia and Lacey had a fight," said Pepper. "But what I didn't tell you was that Zinnia apologized to me last week. And we've been hanging out after school."

Nory was surprised.

"I know you think Zinnia is a spy," Pepper said. "And that would mean she's only been pretending to be my friend." She looked at the ground. "But I can't believe that's true. I *really* don't believe it's true."

Nory replayed what she'd heard yesterday, at Pepper's house. "You two have been going to the playground together?"

"With Taffy and Violet." Pepper squared her shoulders. "Zinnia's fun, Nory. And she's really a good big sister. And she did say sorry. And when I heard Zinnia standing up to Lacey? That was real. Neither of them could have known I was there."

Nory furrowed her brow. "You want me to like Zinnia now?"

Pepper nodded.

Nory felt uncomfortable. "After everything she's done? It's not like she apologized to *me*."

"Will you think about it?" Pepper asked.

Nory sighed. "All right. I'll think about it."

The UDM class had poetry study. And math. And history. Then they had an Upside-Down Magic lesson with more foot painting and more time to clean up. Then they all had a fairly boring discussion of grounding magic and the connections between magic and art. After that, silent reading and a science lesson about dragon biology.

It wasn't until nearly the end of the day that Ms. Starr said they could talk about the Show Off. They all sat in a circle on the carpet.

Willa raised her hand. "I have an idea."

"Let's hear it," said Ms. Starr.

"I can make it rain in small areas now," said Willa. "It doesn't always have to fill the room. So we can do Nory's rain boot dance!"

"What part of *no dancing* doesn't she understand?" Bax wondered aloud.

"Please, Bax. Willa, would you like to show us?" said Ms. Starr. "We'll all be thrilled to see how your control of your talent is developing."

Willa shut her eyes. She breathed deeply. And then it rained . . . only on Bax.

Bax panicked and immediately fluxed into a swivel chair.

"Whoa! Dude!" Elliott said.

"That's what he's been working on in tutoring!" Nory said.

Swivel-Bax began to spin. He zoomed around the room on his wheels. Willa's rain followed him. "I can't make it stop!" Willa cried.

Swivel-Bax banged into Elliott, who jumped in surprise and froze all the water on the floor *and* on the swivel chair. Now there was a pathway of ice where Swivel-Bax had moved, and Swivel-Bax was spinning so fast it made Nory dizzy. She stumbled over to grab him, and *whup!* She slipped on the ice and crashed to the floor.

Willa finally stopped raining.

Swivel-Bax kept spinning.

"Hands in pockets! Hands in pockets!" Ms. Starr cried out.

Elliott shoved his hands in his pockets to prevent them from icing anything else. Marigold had her hands in her pockets, too. It was a technique Ms. Starr had taught them for preventing magical accidents.

Nory tried to get up, but her feet skidded on the ice and . . . *flimp!* She was a bitten: part beaver, part kitten. It was an animal she changed into fairly often when angry or embarrassed.

Bitten-Nory still wanted to help Swivel-Bax, so she leapt up at him and landed smack on the seat of the chair, sending him twirling and skidding across the ice until they both bumped against the wall and stopped short.

There was silence for a moment.

Nory flipped back into girl form. Bax remained a swivel chair.

"Nory, what did I tell you all last week?" asked Ms. Starr.

"Um . . ."

"That friends should not ride friends." Then she burst out laughing.

It was nearly half an hour before Bax got back from the nurse's office, where he had turned back into a boy. Willa apologized to Bax. Only then were they able to hold a productive class meeting.

Nory raised her hand right away, eager to talk about the Show Off before the school day ended.

"I think we should be a band!" she said. "Elliott plays the guitar. Bax plays the piano—right, Bax?"

"I take lessons," Bax admitted. "That doesn't mean I'm any good."

"I play the drums," Andres volunteered.

Marigold bounced in her seat. "I play the clarinet! That's totally enough instruments for a band!"

Bax looked at her. "*You* play an instrument?"

"Yes."

"It's just, you know . . ." He gestured vaguely at Marigold's hearing aid.

"Hearing-impaired people can totally play instruments," said Marigold. "It's just that some instruments are easier than others."

"Oh. Sorry."

"A band," Sebastian said slowly. "We wouldn't

have to use our magic at all." He cocked his head. "But not all of us play something. What would the rest of us do?"

"Pepper's a drummer like Andres—just not with a *drum*," said Nory. "She does, like, body drumming. She's really good!"

Elliott nodded and Nory grinned. They liked her idea! And so many of them could play and sing.

"I can't be in the show. I'd fierce the Fluxers," Pepper said.

"We can figure something out," said Elliott. "If we do a band, we'll have to. We'd need you."

Pepper shook her head. "There'll be Fluxers at the Show Off. And regular animals, too, for the Fuzzies. So, no and no."

Pepper lifted her chin and pressed her lips into a hard line.

Nory wondered, was Pepper mad at Elliott about the Zinnia thing? Or was she truly scared to be in the Show Off?

"You should still think about it," Elliott said to

Pepper. "You're really amazing." He turned to Willa. "And you could make it rain in a tiny area again and have the rain make a pitter-patter sound."

"What if I sing?" Willa said. "I can definitely sing. I was in chorus at my ordinary school!"

"We still need that extra something, though," Elliott said. He snapped his fingers. "Nory! Of course! You can flux into something really unusual!"

"I don't know," Nory said.

"Like a dritten!" said Elliott. "I know you've been practicing your dritten."

"What does a dritten have to do with a band?" Bax asked.

"She could shake the tambourine. In her dritten mouth."

"She would breathe fire on the tambourine! She could breathe fire on the whole school!" Bax said. He saw Dritten-Nory regularly in tutoring with Coach. She couldn't always hold on to her human mind.

"No dritten," Ms. Starr interjected.

"No unusual fluxing," Nory said. "I'll just sing." She gave the group a thumbs-up.

The group paused politely, for about half a second.

"Ooh, ooh, I know!" Marigold said. "She could turn into a flamingo!" She turned to Nory. "You could turn into a beautiful pink flamingo, and you could hold a tambourine in your beak!"

"Yeah, that would count as something special!" Elliott said. "I like it!"

"I don't *do* flamingo," Nory said. "You have to study hard for animals with unusual shapes. And birds aren't easy."

"Or a flamingo-kitten," said Marigold. "A fla-mitten!"

"Or you could say kittingo." Sebastian said, thoughtfully. "Same thing, but sounds better."

"No!" Nory said loudly. She was not going to become a dritten or a kittingo or any sort of mixed-up animal at all, not in front of Father. No way, no how—or, as Pepper put it, *no and NO.*

"Why not?" Elliott asked. "As long as you keep your human mind, it would really make our band stand out."

Nory didn't want to explain about her family and how they wanted to see only typical fluxing from her. Everyone else in UDM had families who seemed to accept them for who they were.

"Nory?" Elliott pressed.

The answer came to her, and she exhaled with relief. "Because of Pepper. Pepper, remember?"

"But Pepper might not be able to be in the Show Off at all, which is why we moved on to *you*," said Andres.

"Pepper's too important," said Nory. "Because seriously, you guys, you haven't seen what she can do. She's, like, genius-level good. Right, Elliott?"

Elliott didn't deny it.

"But Pepper can only perform *if there aren't any animals around*. So it's better if I sing!"

"*No*," everyone said at once.

"Why not? I love singing!"

"Yes," Pepper said, "but just because you love singing doesn't mean . . ." She broke off, looking embarrassed.

"I'll practice a ton," Nory said. "I know all the words already."

"I think what Elliott and Pepper and the others are trying to say is that Willa was in the chorus at her ordinary school, and the kids who play instruments have all taken music lessons," Ms. Starr said gently. "So maybe, if our class does a band, it would make sense to give the people who have been practicing a chance to shine."

"Oh," Nory said. She understood, but her heart sank, because she was back to where she'd started. What was *she* going to do for the Show Off?

At recess the next day, Zinnia sat alone at the top of the climbing structure, far away from Lacey, Rune, and the other Sparkies.

Pepper noticed her right away. She wanted to go say sorry about the way Elliott had yelled and the way Nory had called her a spy and the way she, Pepper, hadn't explained about them being friends. But Elliott and Nory had been so nice about the band yesterday. They had both said they needed her. So Pepper was torn. She knew Elliott would feel she was disloyal if she befriended Zinnia.

It was too much to stand outside, looking at Zinnia all alone, so Pepper went inside early and retreated to the supply closet. There she waited for Ms. Starr to meet her for tutoring, which started when recess was over. She had saved some broccoli from her lunch for Carrot.

Eventually, Ms. Starr came in and set Carrot's box on the floor. "I have a funny request for you, Pepper."

"What is it?"

"I have a friend, an older lady." Ms. Starr sat down and took off her bright orange cardigan. "She is having a problem with mice. Rather than call an exterminator, I was thinking you might help her out. You'd scare them away, but you wouldn't hurt the mice, which an exterminator would. She'd pay you, of course. And it's just over on Oregano Street. I've talked to your father and he's on board. He thought you might like to earn some money with your talent. Maybe Saturday or Sunday? Two o'clock?" Ms. Starr prompted.

"Saturday's the day we practice for the Show Off," said Pepper.

"Are you going to join the show?"

"I want to," Pepper said. "If we can figure out the fiercing."

"Here's an idea. Why don't you just wait in the classroom until it's time for your act?" Ms. Starr said. "If UDM is the last act in the entire show, all Fluxers should be in human form and all animals returned to the Fuzzy room by the time you come to the auditorium. You'll miss watching the other acts, but I think you could safely perform."

"Really?"

"I'll talk to Principal Gonzalez about shifting the schedule to make that happen."

"Thanks!" Pepper said. For a moment she was super excited, but then she remembered: *Nory*.

"But what if Nory wants to flux during the song?" She knew how anxious Nory was about her dad coming to the Show Off. She wanted her friend to have the chance to flux if she wanted to. "If I'm in the band, Nory won't have the option."

Carrot bounded out of the box. "We have an idea for you, Pepper!" the bunny shouted. "It's an idea for pausing your magic!"

Ms. Starr nodded. "It's true. If you can pause your magic for the length of the song, then Nory can flux if she wants to. I did some research and called a couple of experts. Carrot told me that after you scared her on purpose, you seemed to pull your magic back in. Is that true?"

Pepper nodded. "I didn't turn it off. I just stopped pushing it out."

"So let's think of your magic like a river. You were able make it gush out in a big wave, and then you slowed the flow back again, right?"

"Yes," said Pepper. "I think so."

"But it was still flowing," put in Carrot. "It's always still there."

"The professor I spoke to yesterday said that for magic that doesn't turn on and off naturally, like yours and Sebastian's, thinking of it like a river can be very useful," said Ms. Starr. "You won't ever stop a river from flowing, but you can imagine pinching its sides closed for just a minute or two, right? Like a temporary dam."

"I guess I can imagine that," said Pepper.

"Ooh, is that broccoli?" said Carrot, twitching her nose. "Is that broccoli in your pocket?"

Pepper took the broccoli out of her dress pocket.

The rabbit gobbled it up. When Carrot was done, she said, "Okay! Let's try it."

"Try what?" asked Pepper.

"Try pinching your river of magic closed, for a second," said Ms. Starr. "Just a quick pinch. Carrot will be able to feel it if it stops or lessens."

Pepper tried pinching.

"Nothing yet," said Carrot.

"Concentrate, Pepper. Feel the flow of the river of magic inside you," said Ms. Starr. "It should feel like the tickle of your feet when you're foot painting, or the tickle of air when you're nostril breathing, or the rhythm when you're hula-hooping."

Pepper nostril breathed. She felt the magic. The river of the magic.

"Now, can you pinch the sides of it closed?" Ms. Starr asked gently.

Pepper closed her eyes and pinched.

The river stopped flowing. It stopped, and then right away, it hurt. The water was building up against the dam. It hurt, and then the magic exploded out in a rush, breaking through the pinch.

Pepper opened her eyes to find Carrot hiding behind the cat litter again. "Oh, you got me good that time!" said the bunny, laughing as she climbed back out. "I almost upchucked my broccoli!"

"Did I pause my magic?" Pepper asked.

"You did!" said Carrot. "Eloise, I think it paused

for about four seconds before it rushed out and scared me. Did it seem like four seconds to you?"

"Four seconds," Ms. Starr agreed. "Beautiful work, Pepper."

"Can we go back to the cafeteria?" said Carrot. "I want to see what else is in that salad bar."

11

Nory flitted about Aunt Margo's backyard, setting lemonade, chips, and apple slices on the picnic table. The weather was warm even though it was October, so she thought she and the UDM kids could practice their act outside. They could be inspired by nature! They could breathe the fresh air!

Elliott, Sebastian, and Marigold showed up together, with Willa and Andres right behind them. Willa fastened Andres's leash to the picnic table. He was holding bongo drums. Bax arrived with an electronic keyboard. Pepper followed him, pushing the UDM class wheelbarrow with several more of Andres's drums in it.

"I'm learning to put my fiercing on hold," Pepper told Nory. "Just for a couple seconds at a time, but I think it might be a lot longer by the Show Off. In case you want to do kittingo."

Nory shook her head. "Thanks, but I don't even do flamingo. I don't have *anything* but black kitten that I know for sure I can hold for a long time without it getting mixed up. And any fifth-grade Fluxer can already do black kitten, so there's really no point."

What she didn't say was how important it was for her not to do mixed-up animals for the Show Off. There was just no way. Not with Father coming.

"Okay," said Pepper. "But just in case you change your mind, Ms. Starr is helping me work on it."

Elliott came and sat down next to Pepper and Nory. "Zinnia came to my house yesterday," he told them.

"She did?" Pepper said.

"Yeah. She apologized for everything that happened since our magic came in. She said she's been terrified of Lacey and going along with all kinds of bad stuff, but she got the courage to stand up to her after she saw you fierce that swarm of wasps. She feels awful about everything she did now." Elliott sighed. "Then I said sorry about yelling at her the other day, without letting her talk. And then she had a peanut butter cookie in my kitchen and said she wasn't a spy."

Pepper blinked and pressed her lips together. "She got the courage to say no to Lacey because of me?"

Elliott shrugged. "That's what she said."

"And do you believe she's not a spy?"

Elliott shrugged again. "I'm not a hundred percent sure. I'm willing to be friendly with her, but I'm not exactly going to tell her all our secrets. You know?"

"I need a place to put my drums!" Andres called from the end of his leash. "Nory, would your aunt care if we put them on the roof of the garden shed?"

"I'll ask," Nory said.

Aunt Margo said that was fine. They dragged out a ladder and put Andres's collection of drums into a place where he could reach them. Marigold played scales on her clarinet. Bax set up his keyboard on the picnic table, running electricity from inside the house. Elliott sat beside Bax and tuned his guitar. Willa asked Figs for a large bowl of water. She sat at the picnic table and frowned.

"Oh," she finally said, dismayed. "I'm outdoors. I have a cool idea to show you guys, but I can't make my rain cloud here. I can only rain *indoors*."

"I know!" cried Nory. "You can go in the garden shed." She opened the doors to Aunt Margo's tiny shed, which was filled with shovels, flowerpots, and a snowblower.

Willa brought the bowl inside and then was able to make a small and wobbly rain cloud over it. The raindrops fell slow, fast, or medium into the bowl, making different plunking noises. "That's my instrument!" she said happily.

"Wow." Nory was impressed.

"Okay: 'Crazy-Daisy Shame!'" said Elliott. "Andres, want to start us off?"

Andres rapped his drumsticks together. "And a one—and a two—and a one, two, three!" he called.

He pounded out the tempo. After several false tries, Marigold figured out the notes to the melody on the clarinet. Bax played a bass line with his left hand. Elliott joined in, playing what was maybe harmony.

They were playing! And Willa was singing.

Bax riffed on the keyboard with his right hand as well. He wasn't half bad, Nory thought. She looked to Sebastian for confirmation. He had set his tambourine down and was grimacing and waving his hands back and forth.

"No, no, no!" he cried. "You have to stop. You have to stop *now*, I'm begging you!"

Willa stopped singing.

Bax, Elliott, and Marigold let their hands fall. Willa's rain kept slowly pitter-pattering.

Andres gave a final bang to his bongos.

Sebastian put down the tambourine and tore at his hair. "The sound waves are a mess! Elliott's guitar is strangling Bax's keyboard. Bax, when you do that doodly-doodly-doo thing"—he demonstrated with his fingers—"the notes look like ghouls rising from the grave. Also, they don't align with the waves from Marigold's clarinet. The drumbeat is inconsistent, which doesn't help. And the rain is too fast."

"He's kinda right," Pepper said. She winced to say sorry. "I can't see it like Sebastian can, but I can hear it."

"Good music looks beautiful," Sebastian said. "Good music is like looking at a sunrise. You," he said to Andres. "Let Willa start with a slow pitter-pat. Then add in a simple beat."

Willa pitter-patted.

Andres hit a single bongo.

"No, watch my hand, Andres. One. Two. Three. Four. Stay. On. This. Beat." Sebastian moved his hand down, up, to the side, and up. "Bax, skip the doodly-doos for now and just—yep!" he said as Bax started with the bass line. "Okay, let all those three guys come in and then, Pepper, you come in with your percussion. And when I point at you, Marigold and Elliott come in. *After* that first little introduction bit. Not during. After."

"Yessir," Marigold said.

"Ready, and go!" said Sebastian.

Nory listened in growing amazement. What Sebastian said made sense, or it sure sounded as if it did.

He stopped everyone again and gave advice to Willa about vocals, and then turned to Elliott. "Can you sing in tune? Will you do the second verse, then? Bax, I want you to come in on the chorus, too, so it really goes pow! Then we can all sing the third verse together." He had the group try again.

It sounded five thousand times better than it had.

"Yay!" Nory cried. "Oh, yay! Sebastian—you're the conductor! You have to be!"

Sebastian looked proud. He broke a twig off a

tree and tapped it against his palm. "Again, please, people. With feeling."

Using the twig as his conductor's baton, he led the group through Everyday Cake's "Crazy-Daisy Shame" three more times. The third time, he asked Pepper to show him what she could do during the a capella section. He worked with her clapping, layering her beats on top of the others, showing them off.

Nory was thrilled. They were going to be amazing! They were really a band!

It was only when everyone had packed up and gone home that she remembered: She wasn't in it.

And Father was coming.

And Hawthorn.

And Dalia.

They were coming to see her, and Nory had nothing—nothing!—to show off.

12

On Sunday afternoon, Mr. Phan accompanied Pepper to the house of Ms. Starr's elderly friend Mrs. Winterbottom. Mrs. Winterbottom had wrinkly white skin and cotton-ball hair. She was waiting for them by the gate to her front yard when they arrived.

"I do hope you can get rid of these mice," she said, holding on to Pepper's arm for support as she led the way to the porch. "Come along, Mr. Phan. I'll fix you a cup of tea. I have some crochet magazines you can flip through."

Pepper fought not to laugh. Her dad had insisted on coming with her, but Mrs. Winterbottom seemed harmless.

"Oh, I just walked over for the exercise," Pepper's dad said. He frowned and rocked on his heels. "I'll be going now. Pepper? You'll be all right? You can find your way back home?"

"I don't know. Three blocks is a lo-o-ng way."

He grinned. "See you in a bit, then."

"So, how do you do it?" Mrs. Winterbottom asked Pepper once Pepper's dad was gone. They were standing on the porch.

"Scare mice? It comes pretty naturally," Pepper answered. "I have a lot to learn about my magic, but this shouldn't be hard."

"Lucky you," said Mrs. Winterbottom. "I found flaring very tough in school. Finally I realized I'm good at warming things or heating them, but skills like making flames and fireballs will never be easy for me. That's one of the reasons why I became a professional baker." She smiled. "Well, that and a sweet tooth."

Mrs. Winterbottom opened the door to her house and ushered Pepper in. The front room was a living room. The sofa was powder blue, as were the curtains. Mrs. Winterbottom had a great many porcelain figurines, all three inches high.

Okay, Pepper thought. *Now where are the mice?* She tried to push her magic out in a wave like she had in her lesson with Carrot and Ms. Starr.

"My, my!" Mrs. Winterbottom said. "You do have a talent! You don't seem like you're even trying but look, there they go!"

Pepper turned and saw eight small gray mice scurrying from under a bookshelf. She ran to open the front door, and they streaked out in terror. Back in the living room, Mrs. Winterbottom had climbed onto the sofa to save her feet being run over. Four more mice were racing for the door. More and more mice scuttled out from behind the piano and from under a powder-blue armchair. Even more ran down the sides of the bookshelf.

A white mouse with pink eyes took a flying jump from the shelf and landed on a spindly-legged coffee table, rattling the porcelain figurines on top of it.

"Not the girl picking apples! That's a collector's item!" Mrs. Winterbottom cried.

Pepper lunged, steadying the figurine just in time.

Mrs. Winterbottom gasped and pointed at a card table at the other end of the room. "Not the shoe-shine boy! Not the tiny yodeler!"

Pepper righted one figurine and then ran to the next. She steadied a goat herder and a little girl with a bird on her shoulder. A jaunty drummer boy almost fell, but she caught him in time. And the mice kept coming! More and more of them, streaming down the stairs and out of the kitchen.

"Pepper! Help my babies!" Mrs. Winterbottom cried, her head whipping from one tottering figurine to another.

Only when the last mouse made it over the threshold of the door did Mrs. Winterbottom stop squealing.

Then she climbed off the sofa gingerly and gave Pepper a pat on the back.

"My dear girl, you are a wonder," Mrs. Winterbottom said. "I'll recommend you to all my friends. Such magic! Such *powerful* magic!" She insisted on paying Pepper twenty dollars.

The feeling of using her magic to do something helpful was payment enough for Pepper. But she still accepted the money.

Pepper left Mrs. Winterbottom's house walking on clouds. She felt so good, in fact, that she didn't go straight home. She went to Zinnia's house instead.

"I got paid for a job I did," she blurted when Zinnia opened the door. "So I can treat for ice cream. Want to come?"

Zinnia looked at her. "I wasn't sure we were

friends anymore. After what happened when I came over the other day."

"We are," said Pepper decisively. "I just had to work some stuff out. It was cool that you apologized to Elliott."

"It was *so* awkward," said Zinnia, rolling her eyes. "But I feel a bit better now that I did it."

Zinnia told her mom she was going out. She and Pepper chatted as they walked along together. They didn't see the ice-cream truck by the playground, so they walked a couple of extra blocks to the sweet shop in the center of town. Pepper bought a scoop of strawberry ice cream for Zinnia and chocolate for herself. She told Zinnia about Mrs. Winterbottom and the mice.

"You could start a business," Zinnia said. "A non-harmful pest removal service!"

"Maybe I could!" Pepper considered it. Money of her own, to spend as she liked! Money earned by helping people. It sounded good.

As they walked back from the sweet shop,

Pepper and Zinnia passed a poster on the wall out-side the movie theater. It said that Everyday Cake was playing at the Cider Cup Dance Hall in a couple of weeks.

"Do you like Everyday Cake?" asked Zinnia.

"I love them." *Wouldn't it be great if I could earn enough money for tickets?* Pepper thought. She imagined dancing with Zinnia in the audience while the lead singer, Arabelle, belted out "Crazy-Daisy Shame."

"Pepper, hello!" Zinnia was talking.

"Sorry. I was daydreaming."

"I said, there's no way you love Everyday Cake as much as I do. Have you seen my Everyday Cake backpack? I got it when I threw out my *Biscuits BeBop* one. And I have the remix and the regular version of 'Crazy-Daisy Shame.' Also, I have a poster in my bedroom! It's got Arabelle with pink hair."

"Nuh-uh," said Pepper. "I love Everyday Cake even more than you, because I listen to them on my headphones every day when I walk to school."

"No, I love them more because I named my hamster Arabelle."

"No, I love them more because I taught my brothers and sisters how to sing 'Crazy-Daisy Shame' and now my class is doing it for the Show Off!"

Zinnia's eyes went wide. "You are? For the Show Off?"

Pepper clamped her hands over her mouth. "I'm not supposed to tell anyone."

"Don't worry," said Zinnia, licking her ice cream as it dripped down the cone. "Your secret is safe. You can trust me."

Pepper really, really hoped that she could.

13

Nory was excited. And depressed. She was excited that the UDM class would show its school spirit and impress everyone at the Show Off. And she was depressed that all she could do in the act was bang a tambourine. It wasn't enough. Not with Father and Hawthorn and Dalia maybe coming. Now that Sebastian was conducting, Nory was the only one in the whole class who had nothing really musical to offer.

The week leading up to the Show Off was intense. In every classroom, kids ignored their teachers in order to practice their acts. In almost every class-room, the teachers didn't mind, because they wanted their class to win.

Eighth-grade Flyers could be seen practicing floating somersaults in the yard, and the lunch helpers just looked the other way. The seventh-grade Fuzzies were talking nonstop about lizards they'd trained to jump on mini trampolines. Nory and Elliott saw the eighth-grade Fuzzies carrying large fish tanks into their classroom for their squid ballet.

Back on Monday, as the UDM kids practiced their act, Nory had suggested that she be one of the singers again. Everyone had acted like they couldn't hear her.

On Tuesday, she had suggested singing *again*. Same thing.

On Wednesday, Nory got loud. "Why can't I sing lead on the third verse?" she'd shouted. Willa had a verse to sing on her own, and Elliott had one, too. There were *three* verses. Bax only sang backup. Andres, backup as well. Marigold didn't sing, and

Pepper couldn't while doing the body drumming. Why shouldn't Nory sing the third verse on her own?

"Fine," said Sebastian. "Give it a try."

They tried it. Sebastian counted Nory in. Nory breathed deep. She sang the third verse loud and clear.

> *I got my hair soaked!*
> *This is a heart attack!*
> *The earthworms say:*
> *You should love me back!*

Sebastian's hands were over his eyes to block the sound waves. He looked like he was about to pass out.

Nory knew this wasn't a happy sign. She felt heat rush to her face.

Once Sebastian recovered, he said, "I don't want to hurt your feelings, but . . . it's not going to work out, with you singing. There's a pretty large problem with the sound waves."

Nory opened her mouth, wanting to protest. And at the same time, she knew Sebastian wasn't trying to be unkind. He could see the sound waves, and they didn't look good. It was just a fact.

"Am I a bad singer?" she asked, suddenly understanding.

"Yes," Sebastian said. "I'm sorry."

Elliott jumped in. "Nory, you have so many other talents. Like fluxing. What if you were a canary? Then you could tweet."

"Chirp," Sebastian put in. "You could chirp in time to the music. No melody."

"Birds are impressive because they're so hard to do," Bax said encouragingly. "Coach was telling us that yesterday. They don't even teach them until seventh grade, and lots of people don't master them till high school. So everyone would be really wowed if you did canary."

Nory knew Bax was right. Everyone, including Father, would be wowed if she could do canary. But she didn't know how.

"I can't do canary," she confessed.

"Then be another bird!" said Andres. "Be that giant blue thing you fluxed into at the beginning of the year! A bluebird."

Nory blanched. She *had* fluxed into a giant bluebird to save Andres when the Sparkies had endangered him. But the bluebird hadn't lasted long before it went wonky. She had added a touch of elephant to it for size, and then later, well . . . it had ended up the wonkiest animal she had ever done. Heroic, yes. But very, very wonky.

Nory didn't want to think about it. "I don't know if I can do a bird and keep my human mind," she said. "Plus it might go enormous, which would be really embarrassing. And Pepper might scare me, which means the chance of things going wrong is way higher."

"But bluebird could never hurt anyone," said Andres.

"I think we should keep talking about flamingo, if we're talking about birds," put in Marigold.

"Without elephant thrown in, bluebirds are too small; you can barely see them. Flamingos are big and special on their own. And beautiful. You could dance!"

"You could work on flamingo with Coach," said Bax to Nory.

"I can definitely pause my fiercing for thirty seconds now," added Pepper. "I've been practicing every day in case you decided you wanted to flux."

Ms. Starr called over from her desk. "Pepper and I can practice even harder, if Nory wants to flux. Thirty seconds is a good start, and I'm pretty sure she'll be able to go longer soon."

"Can you really, Pepper?" asked Nory. She surged with hope. If she could do an advanced animal like flamingo during the Show Off, *and* keep her human mind the whole time, Father might actually be proud.

She was going to find Coach that very afternoon. It was time for a bonus tutoring session.

14

I need to change into a flamingo," Nory told Coach in his office. "A bright pink flamingo with nothing wonky about it. And maybe I could chirp? If flamingos chirp." She swallowed. "Do you think I can do it?"

"You want to learn flamingo right now?" Coach said, putting down a homemade thistledown muffin.

"It's for the Show Off. And it's really important to me, so yes, I need to start learning it now. Will you help?"

"If I can," Coach said. He stood, brushed the crumbs from his shorts, and blew a sharp blast on his whistle. "Tell me this. Have you ever done a bird of any kind?"

"Once I did bluebird," Nory said. "But it turned very, very wonky."

He brewed them both cups of herbal tea. "It takes the seventh graders two months to get wings when they start studying birds," he said. "But you, you've already done wings, with your bluebird and your dritten, so that part should progress very quickly. And tell me, did your bluebird have a beak? Beaks are difficult."

"It had a beak for a little while," Nory said.

"Any beak at all is very hopeful," said Coach. "I have eighth graders who can't put a beak on their birds. And what about feathers?"

"I had good feathers."

"Were they nice and blue? Some people have trouble with bright-colored birds like flamingos and bluebirds, canaries, cardinals, that kind of thing.

They generally start with sparrows to avoid the color challenge."

"People knew I was a bluebird, for sure," said Nory.

"Then I think I can help you," said Coach. "Yes, yes, I think we can fast-track your flamingo."

For several minutes, he studied her. He asked Nory to flap her arms like wings. He inquired about the shape of her toes. He asked if she'd been eating seaweed snacks and how much fruit she ate each day.

"Righty-o, then," Coach finally said. "Up onto my shoulders!"

"What?"

Coach bent down. "Stand on the chair. Now take my hands . . . good. Now I want you to stand on my shoulders. That's it! Good girl!"

Nory's body wobbled. Her feet were perched on Coach's shoulders. She clutched his big hands as tightly as she could. He raised his arms high, which allowed her, more or less, to stand.

"Ready?" he called.

"What? No!" Nory cried, thinking, *Ready for what?*

"On three!" Coach pronounced. "One, two—"

"PleaseIdon'tthinkthisis—"

"Three!" Coach cried, and he released Nory's hands while at the same time rapidly bending and straightening his legs to bump her off him.

Wheee!

Ouch.

When Nory opened her eyes, Coach's big head was leaning over her. His face was full of concern. "Are you all right?" he said. "Can you hear me? Here, have some pomegranate juice."

Nory gingerly pushed herself to a sitting position. She was in girl form, exactly as she had been when Coach lifted her high on his shoulders. Only now she had a sore bottom.

She chose not to share that with Coach. "I didn't turn into a flamingo, did I?" she said.

"No. You didn't flux at all," Coach said. He scratched his nose. "Bummer. That's a technique we use for the seventh graders who are having a hard time with the birds. It kind of shocks them into fluxing. They do it out of necessity. Ooh, hey, maybe if I lifted you onto my shoulders and then I stood on my desk—"

"No!" Nory said. "I mean, thank you for the offer."

Coach looked disappointed. "Well, your call." He rubbed the back of his neck. "Tell you what. Let's try another technique. Follow me, Nory!"

Nory trotted behind Coach as he strode out of his office and down the hall, then down another hall, until they reached a large room she'd never been in before.

"It's Ms. Fitsnickle's eighth-grade tropical animal room," Coach said, rapping on the door. "Let's see if she has any flamingos you can meet, shall we? For some Fluxers, all it takes is a face-to-face connection."

A short lady shaped like a ball appeared. "Yes?" A grin spread over her round face. "Why, Coach! Can I help you?"

Coach spelled out what they wanted.

Ms. Fitsnickle beckoned them into the room.

Wow.

The room was large and bursting with hot steam. It was filled with animals used for eighth-grade Fuzzy lessons. Nory wanted to soak it all in—the families of lizards, the colorful butterflies, the baby alligator napping on a bed of grass—but Ms. Fitsnickle hustled them toward a small indoor pond behind a fence. It was like a kiddie pool, but nicer. "I have six flamingos!" she said. "Aren't they marvelous?"

They were. Pink and long-legged and beautiful. Nory marveled at their long S-shaped necks and their sticklike legs. They pecked and nibbled at something slimy on the bottom of their pen, and Ms. Fitsnickle explained that it was a mix of algae and the pink shrimpish creatures the flamingos liked to eat.

I like shrimp, Nory thought. *And if I were a flamingo, I could eat shrimp every day. Yum.*

And just like that . . . *snibble-pipple-pop!* Nory's neck stretched, her legs turned skinny and long, and feathers sprouted over every inch of her. And, as part of it all, she *pinkened*. She actually felt herself pinken!

"Now we have seven flamingos!" Ms. Fitsnickle exclaimed. "Fabulous!"

· "Nory, you did it!" Coach cried. "The beak and everything—brilliant, my girl!"

Shrimp, Flamingo-Nory thought. *Shrimp, shrimp, shrimp. Shrimpish things. Must gobble shrimpish things!*

"Darling, no!" Ms. Fitsnickle said as Flamingo-Nory lifted one gawky leg into the pen. "This is *their* pen! You are a fluxed student. They don't like outsiders! Oh, dear, Coach. She doesn't have the human mind right now, does she?!"

Shrimpy-shrimpy-yum-yum-yum, Flamingo-Nory thought. Then hands were swatting at her, and a human thing was talking loudly to her—a bald human thing—and the other flamingos were hissing. At her! The nerve!

"You need to get hold of your human mind!" cried the ball-shaped human.

Shrimpies, here I come!

Flamingo-Nory flapped her mighty wings, and her beak started to twitch and wait, was that fur sprouting on her wings? Was she adding kitten to her flamingo? *Oh, no!*

Her pink wings flopped. Noises rushed in, Coach became Coach and Ms. Fitsnickle became Ms. Fitsnickle, and *fwoomp*. She was Nory again.

Coach grinned. "Magnificent flamingo. Magnificent! For all of"—he checked his stopwatch—"thirteen seconds!"

"I've heard of only one Dunwiddle Fluxer who's ever pulled off a flamingo," Ms. Fitsnickle said. "And he was an eighth grader! You must be in the . . . sixth grade? Seventh?"

"Fifth," Nory said shyly.

"Zamboozle! Your magic is strong, young lady!" She pulled her eyebrows together. "Although, for a moment there . . ." She tapped her lip. "Coach, did you see a bit of . . . hmm, how to say it . . ."

"I saw something, yes." He gazed at Nory. "There was the slightest tremor, the briefest of ripples . . . you were most definitely a flamingo. But then I think you might have added a bit of—perhaps—*kitten* there at the end?"

Yes. She'd felt it. Kittingo. She didn't want to be a kittingo!

Ms. Fitsnickle looked curious, then gave a curt nod. "Birds require practice, that's all."

"If I practice a ton, do you think I could hold it for longer?" Nory asked. "Without adding in kitten?"

"Vanity helps with flamingos," said Coach. "With birds generally, but especially with flamingos. You might try admiring yourself in the mirror. The flamingo part of your brain will appreciate it. Let that be your homework."

Ms. Fitsnickle guided them to the door, a clear signal that she was ready for them to clear out.

"Thank you, Cordelia," Coach said, shaking Ms. Fitsnickle's hand.

"Thank you, and thank the flamingos," said Nory.

"Oh, it's all in a day's work," said Ms. Fitsnickle.

• • •

Nory turned into a flamingo twice on her walk home. She knew she wasn't supposed to. You had to get a license to flux in public spaces, and each animal was licensed separately. But she was so excited she couldn't help it. As she walked, she thought vain flamingo thoughts. *Everyone is admiring my pinkness.* Or *I have the longest legs of any flamingo in my neighborhood.*

Even with the vain thoughts, she did keep popping back to girl shape after only a few seconds. And the second time she fluxed, something definitely felt furry around the tail. She could not become a kittingo at the Show Off. She could NOT.

Nory looked on the bright side. It wasn't perfect yet, but she could do flamingo. She'd get better and better each time. By the time of the Show Off, she'd be a fifth grader with skills more advanced than every sixth grader. Every seventh grader! Almost every eighth grader!

She'd be Flamingo-Nory, and Father would be proud.

• • •

For the next two days, Nory worked on her flamingo. She could hold it for longer and longer, but during band practice, when Pepper's control ran out and the fiercing magic surged, Nory's flamingo wonked out. Her flamingo neck shrank, and she grew whiskers. Or she sprouted a kitten tail.

Even if Pepper didn't start fiercing, there were problems. As soon as Nory tried to feel the music and dance, she'd lose control of the bird. Her feathers would turn to fur, or she'd swell up to the size of an elephant and her beak would transform into an elephant trunk. She had knocked over Elliott's guitar twice, and had whacked Bax in the face with a giant wing three times. What was wrong with her? Why couldn't she just keep that flamingo shape, or at least flux directly back into a girl?

Still, the UDM band continued practicing.

Pepper practiced a complicated percussion sequence that happened during the a capella section of the song. She also practiced pausing her magic with Carrot and Ms. Starr.

Bax practiced piano playing and vocal harmonies. He only fluxed into a rock once. Unfortunately, he broke the piano bench in the process.

Marigold practiced clarinet parts. She shrank one of the keys, but she could still press it with her pinkie.

Willa practiced her small rain cloud and the first verse. She had to change into a dry outfit only once. Bax had to twice.

Elliott practiced the second verse and guitar parts. He froze a few of the strings, but the ice melted by the next morning.

Andres tried practicing while drumming his heels against the ceiling to keep a steady beat. But Sebastian screamed, "My eyes! My eyes! Make it stop!" So Andres quit with his heel beats.

Sebastian didn't practice. He just acted like he knew everything. But he did borrow a real baton from the music teacher.

They all practiced headstands, because Ms. Starr made them. "Good for integrating the body and mind. That's a vital part of using upside-down magic to its best potential!" she cried.

The night before the Show Off, Nory couldn't sleep. She needed to do a perfect, regular flamingo for more than two minutes and eleven seconds—that was how long the song was. Pepper needed to hold her fiercing for that long, too.

Nory sat up in bed. She had to try it again.

She turned on the radio, quietly, so as not to wake Aunt Margo. Some dance music came on—nothing as good as Everyday Cake, but it would do for practicing. Then she stood on her bed. She flapped her arms. She visualized the flamingo. She jumped.

Before she hit the ground, her arms started to tingle. Her body crackled and shrank. Her neck stretched and grew. Pink feathers covered her skin. Flamingo!

Flamingo-Nory could see herself in the mirror behind her door.

Ooh, she looked *good*. She had been practicing in

the mirror a lot, of course, because vanity really did help her hold on to the flamingo longer. It seemed to help her keep her human mind in control, too.

Such a lovely curved beak. So pinky pink pink. Such sleek feathers.

But could she stay a flamingo for the whole two minutes and eleven seconds she needed for the show? Without going wonky?

Flamingo-Nory took deep breaths. She held still, despite the music. Totally still, with one leg tucked up, flamingo fashion. She looked back and forth between the clock and her mirror.

She admired herself for one minute and fifteen seconds. She admired herself for one minute and *thirty* seconds.

Ooh, the music has such a good beat, though. It would be so much fun to shake these flamingo legs. It might even feel good to grow some kitten whiskers and a tail . . .

No! Don't dance. Stay a bird. Look how beautiful you are! Hold still!

Two minutes! *Two minutes and eleven seconds,* and still she stayed 100 percent beautiful, lovely, perfect flamingo! Flamingo-Nory had done it! Hooray!

Slowly and carefully, she fluxed back into a girl.

Okay, then. She couldn't dance as a flamingo. She couldn't really move, at all, if she wanted to avoid going wonky. But who cared?!

Not Nory.

She had stayed in full bird form—and a brightly colored, eighth-grade-level bird at that—and that was what mattered for the Show Off.

15

Then, finally, it was here. The night of the Show Off.

Pepper was so nervous she was afraid she might yak.

"Just breathe," Zinnia told her. They were alone in Ms. Starr's room. Pepper had to stay there until it was time for the UDM performance, so that she wouldn't scare any Fluxers or animals. Zinnia wasn't in the Show Off, so she was keeping Pepper company.

"Okay." Pepper tried to take a deep, slow breath, but it didn't happen.

"Maybe you should stop pacing," Zinnia said.

Zinnia would be leaving soon to go watch some of the performances. She didn't want to miss the whole thing. When UDM was up—they were last in the whole show—she'd run and fetch Pepper. It was a small job, but a crucial one. Pepper had argued hard to get Elliott to trust Zinnia with it, and he'd finally agreed. The rest of them would be too busy getting ready for their number.

Pepper walked the length of Ms. Starr's room. She reached the wall with the windows, tagged the windowsill, and turned around to retrace her steps.

"Think about something else," Zinnia said. "How's your pest-removal service going? Have you gotten any more jobs?"

Pepper had, actually. She'd earned thirty-five dollars by channeling a colony of ants out of Mr. Bittle's kitchen and into his garden. She'd earned *fifty* dollars for ridding Maisy Brown's apple trees of worms. "I've earned eighty-five more dollars," she said. "And I have three more jobs lined up!"

Zinnia whistled. "Wow."

Pepper grinned. "I have a plan. I was going to make it a surprise, but I can't. It's too exciting."

"What is it?" asked Zinnia.

"I want to buy Everyday Cake tickets. For you and me! We'll see Arabelle in person! I'll have enough for three tickets if I just do one more job. You, me, and a parent. Remember the sign? They're playing at Cider Cup next weekend."

Zinnia's face fell. "Oh, no, Pepper. That's not going to work."

"Why not?"

"The Everyday Cake concert is sold out. It's been sold out for months. My mom tried to get me tickets for my birthday!"

"What? No!"

"Yeah, it's true."

"But they have posters up *every*where," said Pepper.

"So people will buy the new album," said Zinnia. "That's what my mom said."

Zwingo. Pepper sighed. "What'll I do with all my money?"

"I don't know," said Zinnia. "But on the plus side, you're rich!" She checked the clock in the classroom. "Listen. I'm going to go watch for a little bit and then I'll come back and get you. Are you going to be okay? Can you really pause your fiercing?"

"The song is two minutes and eleven seconds," said Pepper. "Yesterday I did it! I pinched it off for the whole time. But that was the first time ever that I made it that long. I *think* I should be okay. Unless I'm nervous and mess it up. Oh, Zinnia, I'm nervous I'll be nervous."

"You're going to be amazing," Zinnia said. "I know it."

Nory's heart thumped as she peeked through the red velvet curtains. The auditorium was packed. Every seat was filled. The show was running. It was almost time for the fifth-grade acts that ended the program.

Father, Hawthorn, and Dalia were late.

They weren't in the audience. They probably weren't even coming.

Dalia had only said *maybe*.

Nory hoped they were coming.

No, she hoped they weren't coming.

No, she hoped they *were* coming.

Why were they late? The entire Show Off was nearly over.

They weren't coming.

Elliott touched her shoulder. "Hi."

"Elliott!" Nory whispered. "Look how many people there are! I see your family in the front row!" His dad was pointing an enormous camera at the stage. His mom was holding a bouquet of flowers. His baby brother was asleep.

"They are so embarrassing," Elliott complained. "Is your family here?"

"No." She swallowed and briefly closed her eyes. "Aunt Margo is here with Figs. But not the rest of them."

"Forget your dad. Come watch with the rest of us," Elliott urged.

Nory hesitated, then followed her friend. The janitor had set up a cluster of foldout chairs for the kids backstage. Right now, it was filled with fifth graders. After each class finished its act, the students joined the general audience.

Nory sat on a metal chair. She had a clear view of the well-lit stage, where a spotlight illuminated the fifth-grade Flyers. Each person was dressed all in white and held a flag. They were attempting to fly in a synchronized pattern while twisting the flags and waving them back and forth. Folk music blared from the sound system.

"What are they doing?" Nory whispered to Elliott.

Lacey Clench, wearing a very strange hat, whipped around from the row in front of them. "Shhh!"

"It's a traditional Flyer Flag Dance of the Harvest Season," Elliott whispered. He had a program in his hand.

Nory squinted. "Won't their flags get dirty, dragging on the ground like that?"

"I think they're supposed to be flying higher. And not so crooked." Some of the Flyers were nicely vertical, but others were on the diagonal, and a couple had their knees bent and their feet wide apart.

There was a gasp from the audience as one of the Flyers dropped to the floor and started crying.

"I'm guessing that wasn't on purpose," Elliott whispered.

Lacey whipped around again. "The Flyer Flag Dance of the Harvest Season is an important legacy of the Flyers around the world! My nonna is a Flyer, so stop being disrespectful!"

Nory gulped.

Next up were the fifth-grade Fuzzies. Their act involved a camel.

They took turns commanding it, only it wouldn't do much.

"Behold!" a nervous-looking Fuzzy cried, flinging one hand high in the air.

The camel worked its lips. Then it yawned.

"Be*hold*!" the girl said again. Then she spoke in a low, angry voice to the camel. "Riverdance! Riverdance! Come on!"

The camel stood there.

Other kids tried to get the camel to listen, but it didn't Riverdance, or leap, or do anything else except yawn.

Finally, the camel flattened its ears, pulled back its upper lip, and hocked a huge, globby loogie smack onto one boy's face. The audience broke into a smattering of confused applause.

Next up were the fifth-grade Flickers. Their act was called Oranges Away! The Flickers wore sailor outfits and held a dozen oranges, which they waved around in patterns. Oranges over the heads! Oranges behind the backs! Oranges under the knees! Tossing oranges back and forth.

Nory guessed the oranges were supposed to appear and reappear in sync with one another, but they didn't. Every now and then one of them went invisible, but most of the Flickers were too nervous to get their magic working well.

Next were the fifth-grade Fluxers—and there was no denying it: They rocked "Kitty Grooves."

Kitten backspins. Kitten whips and kitten nae naes. The butterscotch kittens leapt over the black kittens' backs. The black kittens pounced while the butterscotch kittens wiggled their backsides like they were getting ready to pounce. They popped and locked. They stomped their paws and shook their tails. They even shook their ears.

Now Nory was nervous. The UDM kids could probably beat the Flyers, the Flickers, *and* the Fuzzies. But these Fluxers? They were tough competition.

And now it was time for the fifth-grade Flares. The spotlight went dark. All music ceased, until a low, throbbing drumbeat started up. Onstage, what looked like a purple firefly flared a purple light. Nory leaned closer. It was Rune, one of the Sparkies. He wore a purple bodysuit with purple wings. Strapped around his waist was a small metal cage filled with cotton balls.

"He's lighting the cotton balls on fire one by one," Elliott said. "But he's controlling the heat of the fire! He's keeping just to the purple spectrum!"

A Flare dressed in green fluttered onto the stage, adorned with a similar metal cage full of cotton balls. She used her magic to set the cotton balls on fire— keeping to the green part of the heat spectrum.

The effect was spectacular. Dark stage; low, steady drumming; and purple and green fireflies twinkling on and off. A pink firefly entered stage left. From stage right, a blue firefly twirled into sight. They danced and flared and swooped their arms— and tiny flames flared from their fingertips, matching the colors of their costumes.

Lacey twirled onto the stage. She wore a head-piece with seven sparklers on top, and each sparkler burned a different color. Was she queen of the fireflies?

She looked incredible.

Nory snuck back over to the far side of the curtain to peek at the audience. She put her eye to a split in the fabric, and her blood seemed to reverse directions in her veins.

He was here. Father was here!

He was standing on the side—too late to get a seat—but he had a good view. Dalia and Hawthorn stood on either side of him.

Nory darted back to Elliott. "My father's here!" she whispered.

Elliott gave her a thumbs-up. Nory began to wheeze.

She hadn't seen Father since he'd sent her away.

He had sent her purple rain boots, but he hadn't actually *said* anything.

And now she was going to try flamingo in front of him! With Pepper the Fierce standing next to her!

Sure, she had held flamingo for two minutes and eleven seconds the night before, but only that one time. What if Pepper fierced? What if Nory couldn't keep still with "Crazy-Daisy Shame" playing and turned into something wonky?

"Elliott." She shook him. "Elliott! I can't! I can't go out onstage, not with my father in the audience!"

"Yes, you can," Elliott said. "Do you want to try a headstand to calm you down?"

"No!"

"Do you want a choco fire truck?"

"No! Elliott!" Nory shook him again.

"What about some deep breathing? Or a glass of water? Really, Nory. It's going to be all right."

"Let's get ready," said Bax from behind Nory. "We're up next."

The UDM kids convened in the prop room, which had a soundproof door. The school piano was in there, on wheels. They had to push it onstage after the Flares finished, then set up their other instruments.

Andres had his drums attached to a board on the end of a long pole that they'd also bring onstage. The drums were the right height for him to play when his leash was attached to Bax's piano stool. Willa had her bowl of water covered with a large sheet of plastic wrap. Marigold unpacked her clarinet from its case.

"Where's Zinnia?" Elliott said. "It's almost time for her to get Pepper."

"I'm here," Zinnia said, slipping into the room.

From the other side of the door, Nory heard a roar of enthusiastic applause for the Flares. It went on forever.

Father was out there.

"I can't," Nory moaned, covering her face with her hands. "I can't compete with 'Kitty Grooves'! Or the Fireflies!"

Elliott dug in his backpack for his water bottle. "Here. I'll make you an ice pack. That'll help you calm down. You need to keep cool and calm. Then everything will be okay. Let me just freeze this for you." He concentrated, and soon came the *snap* of newly formed ice. "Oh, *NO*."

Sebastian gasped. "Elliott, what have you done?"

Nory looked up.

Elliott hadn't iced the bottle. He'd iced the instruments.

"My clarinet is frozen!" Marigold wailed. "I can't play a frozen clarinet!"

"If I play my drums, they'll shatter!" said Andres.

The guitar was covered in frost. Even the piano was completely iced. So was Willa's bowl.

"Oh, no, oh, no, oh, no," Elliott cried.

The door to the prop room burst open. The Flares spilled in. They were happy and glowing and full of high spirits.

"Your turn," Lacey sang to Nory. "Beat that, Nory Horace!" She stopped and took in the frozen instruments. Then she exploded in laughter. The other Sparkies joined in.

"Omigosh," Lacey cackled. "You guys are such wonkos!"

"You *froze* your instruments?" Rune said. "Why?"

"Zinnia, go get Pepper!" Elliott said desperately. "If we don't have instruments, at least we have her!"

Lacey's eyebrows shot up. She blocked Zinnia's way. "Zinnia! Are you seriously helping them?"

Zinnia blinked.

"Please get Pepper," Elliott repeated. "If we have her percussion, maybe we can still perform."

Zinnia stepped toward the door.

"If you get Pepper right now, you will never be a Sparky again," Lacey warned.

Zinnia froze, her eyes wide.

"Zinnia," Elliott said.

Zinnia's struggle played out on her face. "Both of you, stop! I don't want to pick sides. Why do I have to pick sides?"

"Because you do," Nory said. "Enough is enough."

16

ack in Ms. Starr's classroom, Pepper heard the deep throb of the Flares' music. It made the windowpanes shake. She ran to the door, peering down the empty hall.

She heard wild applause and balled her hands into fists. Where was Zinnia? Zinnia was supposed to come get her when it was time for the UDM act. If the Flares were done, then it was time!

But Pepper wasn't supposed to go without her. Zinnia was supposed to get an all clear from Ms. Starr, and Ms. Starr was getting an all clear from

Ms. Fitsnickle that the animals were safely put away. Ms. Fitsnickle was getting an all clear from Coach that the Fluxers were in human form.

What was happening?

Something must have gone wrong. It was time for the final number. Pepper's friends had to be waiting for her.

She decided not to wait for the all clear.

She ran down the hall to the back entrance of the auditorium. From there, she could enter the prop room. She burst in.

The Sparkies were laughing, all of them. The UDM kids looked small and shocked, with the exception of Bax, who looked angry. And Zinnia . . .

Pepper swayed.

Zinnia, an excellent Flare for her age, stood before the school piano, hands outstretched and fingertips sparking.

Was she—?

She was!

She was trying to burn up the piano!

"Stop!" Pepper wailed. "Zinnia, no!"

Zinnia jumped. She saw Pepper, and it seemed as though a jolt pulsed through her and made her magic even stronger.

The piano burst into flames.

Wood crackled. Wires popped. Black and white keys flew into the air like a scattered deck of cards.

It burned bright and was over in seconds.

The piano was gone. Nothing remained but a smoking spot on the floor and a few sad keys.

Everything in Pepper's stomach turned sour. What a good little actress Zinnia was! She sure had fooled Pepper. "All along I defended you," she told Zinnia, barely able to control her voice.

Zinnia pretended to look anguished. "Pepper, I—"

"Destroyed the piano!" Pepper said. "We need the piano! You know that because you got me to tell you what our act was." She started to shake.

"Pepper!" Zinnia tried.

Spots clouded Pepper's vision. She felt light-headed. "You were never my friend! You were a spy! You *used* me!"

Pepper swiped at her tears, furious at herself for caring, even now. She pointed at the door and said, "Leave! You are a horrible person, Zinnia Clarke. I never want to talk to you again!"

A shocked silence fell over the room.

Zinnia muffled a cry—*such* a good little actress—and fled the room.

"I think Pepper made Zinnia's decision for her now. Wouldn't you say?" Lacey spoke blandly. "It doesn't matter what Zinnia *wanted* to do, my Sparkies, because she's obviously not going to be friends with these UDM wonkos after *that*." She took off her sparkler headdress. "Rune, go after Zinnia and act like you're worried about her. Later we can welcome her back to the Sparkies, but not until she pays for her mistakes."

"How will she pay?" asked Rune.

"Oh, we'll make her *do* something," said Lacey. "Something *creative*. It'll be fun."

Pepper didn't understand. *Pay for her mistakes? Welcome her back to the Sparkies?* If all along, Zinnia had been a spy, then why would she have to pay for her mistakes? Why keep up the act now?

"She was trying to help us," Nory told Pepper. "She wasn't a spy. Lacey told Zinnia she had to choose between us and them. And Elliott and I said the same thing. Which we probably shouldn't have." She looked uncomfortable, but then she squared her shoulders and lifted her chin. "But Zinnia chose us."

The world shifted beneath Pepper's feet.

"I froze all our instruments," Elliott confessed. "I panicked. Nory was freaking out, so I wanted to make her a cold pack, and my magic went wild because I was nervous. But Zinnia melted the ice on Andres's drums and Willa's water bowl. And on my guitar and Marigold's clarinet. She burned the piano, but she saved everything else."

The seventh-grade flare teacher popped his head

into the prop room. "Curtain time, kids," he said briskly. "Oh, hello. What's this? Why didn't anyone use a fire extinguisher? That's really basic safety, you guys." He stepped over to the wall and sprayed the last of the smoking floor.

"Guys, we have to go on," Andres said.

"He's right," Nory said. "My father is out there."

Marigold and Pepper spoke at the same time. "But—"

"Zip it," Elliott said. "I agree with Andres. We're going on." He looked at Sebastian. "Right?"

Sebastian straightened his spine. He was the conductor, the leader of the band.

"Let's do this thing!" he said.

17

Pepper's head spun.

She had betrayed Zinnia, not the other way around.

Sebastian pushed her toward the stage, his hand between her shoulder blades. Elliott was already on, along with Marigold, Willa, and Andres. They had brought the instruments (except the piano, which didn't exist anymore) and attached Andres's leash to the chair Marigold sat in. Mics were set up for the singers.

Everyone looked nervous in the glare of the lights. Sweat shone on Elliott's upper lip. He kept changing the way he held his guitar, as if it had turned into a foreign object when he wasn't looking.

The crowd was huge, a shadowed mass of heads, faces, and bodies.

"They're waiting for us to start," Sebastian said to Pepper in the wings. "Go on. Take your place."

Pepper dug her heels into the floor. "I don't think I can."

Sebastian spoke firmly. "You're fine. You're also the star of our act. *Go*."

"Are you worried you won't be able to control your fiercing?" Nory whispered.

Pepper nodded. "Really worried. After everything that's happened, I'm not feeling grounded."

"I'm worried I won't be able to play the piano, since Zinnia burned it to a crisp," Bax said darkly.

"Maybe you can!" Nory said. "Do what Coach told you!"

Pepper didn't know what Nory was talking about.

"Listen," Nory whispered. "I'll stay human. Okay, Pepper? And then you won't have to worry about fiercing. Just do your music."

"But, Nory—" Sebastian said.

"Nope, it's settled," Nory said. Pepper thought she looked relieved. "I don't need to be a flamingo. I'm happy to go as just me. I'm totally fine with it. Then the fiercing doesn't matter, and we will all be amazing." She bent and picked up the tambourine. "I'll play the tambourine! And I won't sing! It'll be great!"

"All right then, it's decided. Let's go," Sebastian told Pepper, Nory, and Bax. "Come on."

He strode onto the stage. Pepper, Nory, and Bax followed.

"We need a piano," Bax muttered. "We need. A. Piano. This is a disaster."

"Do what you're working on with Coach!" Nory

repeated. She plastered a big smile on her face and took the mic. "Hello! We are the fifth-grade Upside-Down Magic class!" she said, loud and clear. "And we're proud to rock the Dunwiddle Show Off!"

Sebastian raised his baton and let it drop.

Andres opened up on the bongos.

Willa started her rain and a few people in the audience cheered. A light shone on the bowl. The raindrops kerplopped together to make a beat.

And they went on. Drumming and kerplopping.

Nothing else happened.

This was where Bax usually came in on piano.

But Bax stood there, looking miserable, doing nothing.

Pepper couldn't start till she heard Bax's bass line. What was she supposed to do?

Elliott gulped and started up on his guitar, but it didn't sound right without the piano.

Marigold gamely joined in on her clarinet. Same thing.

Sebastian made a pained expression.

Pepper didn't know when to come in. Her cue usually came from Bax's bass line.

She glanced back at Bax. He drew his eyebrows together, and Pepper had a sudden and awful suspicion that he was going to flux into a rock just to get himself out of this horrible, embarrassing situation.

Bax's face grew red. The tendons on his neck bulged.

BOOM DING-A-CLANG-CLANG!

The audience gasped, and then broke into spontaneous applause.

Bax had fluxed into a piano. *A piano!*

Not only that, but a *player* piano! That was what it looked like, as the black and white keys went up and down. The bass line to "Crazy-Daisy Shame" echoed through the auditorium.

It wasn't really a player piano, though. It was Piano-Bax. And he was playing himself!

The applause was so loud that Sebastian made

the "stop" motion with his baton. The UDM kids all stopped playing. Piano-Bax heard them and stopped, too. They waited until the cheers died down, and they started the number again.

First Andres's drumbeat. Then Willa's rain.

Then the piano bass line.

Happiness welled up inside Pepper, and there was her cue! She clapped, slapped, and snapped, driving the music forward with an addictive percussive beat.

Elliott came in on the guitar, and Marigold on clarinet.

Willa sang the first verse into her microphone.

During the first chorus, Elliott took a break from the guitar to dip his hand into Willa's bowl of water. He drew out icicles—one, two—and tossed them to Pepper. She caught them! And played them by beating them together. The ice sparkled.

Andres floated gently beside his drums, his white sneakers high above what ordinary fifth-grade Flyers could manage.

Nory was proud of her friends. So proud. Everyone was finally admiring the special magic of Bax Kapoor! And the indoor rain of Willa Ingeborg. Sebastian was using his Upside-Down Flicker talent while conducting, and Elliott had used his ice power.

The band hit the third verse. The singers sang it together, a capella. Then their voices stopped, and it was just Pepper and the rain.

The crowd went wild.

When the instruments kicked back in, Pepper leaned toward Nory.

"Go for it," Pepper whispered in Nory's ear. "I know I can pause my fiercing till the end of the song. It's less than thirty seconds. No problem."

Nory knew it was true. She raised her eyebrows at Sebastian, who was conducting. "Do it!" he mouthed. "Flamingo."

Nory set down her tambourine and focused.

Her muscles shivered. Her spine popped. Her neck stretched.

She was Flamingo-Nory: a super-good-looking, sleek and long-legged, bright pink flamingo.

There was a smattering of applause.

Flamingo-Nory felt her body start to sway to the music and made herself stay perfectly still. She couldn't risk moving and messing it up.

All around her, her friends were smiling and playing and enjoying the moment. They were showing off their unusual magics. And the audience was loving it. Even Hawthorn and Dalia were dancing and waving their hands in the air.

Father, however, stood with his arms folded across his chest. Flamingo-Nory saw him frown at her and her friends. His face was downright sour.

He *still* wasn't impressed? Even though she was a perfect flamingo? *Why not? Can't he see how magnificent we all are?* Flamingo-Nory wondered. *What is wrong with him?*

Then her beak dropped open. She had never thought of it like that.

Something *was* wrong with him.

With *him*. Maybe the problem had been with Father all along.

Flamingo-Nory wanted to dance. She wanted to have fun. She wanted to enjoy herself. "Crazy-Daisy Shame" was her favorite song!

She wanted to wonk out.

She let her feathers become fur and her beak become a kitten nose. Her whiskers sprouted, and then her whole head became a kitten head. Her neck shrank, and her body was a kitten body with a nice fluffy tail. She kept her two marvelous flamingo legs and added two more at the front, since she no longer had wings. She stayed her bright flamingo-pink color, and she danced and waggled and shook herself all around.

"What is she?" someone from the audience cried.

"A pink kitten!" someone yelled.

"With flamingo legs!" someone else said.

Sebastian flung his arms in Nory's direction. The band pulled back to just Willa on rain and Andres on drums. "Ladies and gentlemen!" Sebastian proclaimed, addressing the audience in a booming voice. "The one . . . the only . . . kittingo!"

The band sang the final chorus while Kittingo-Nory danced her heart out.

> *Don't don't don't*
> *It's a crazy-daisy shame*
> *Don't keep your honey bunch*
> *Out in the rain*
> *Open that door*
> *I'll come in and get dry*
> *Don't don't don't*
> *Don't pass me by!*

When their act finally ended, everyone in the audience jumped to their feet, applauding and whistling.

Well, everyone except Father. He was already standing. And he didn't applaud.

Still. The Flares had been good, with their Fireflies of Many Colors act. And the Fluxers had been good, too, with "Kitty Grooves." But Kittingo-Nory and her friends had been better than good. They'd been fabulous.

Kittingo-Nory swished her tail and took in all the people who were standing, stomping, and clapping. She and her friends had done it.

They had shown everyone just how wonderful upside-down magic could be.

18

Pepper went to the reception hall with the others, feeling shy at first and then astonished—and happy. Kid after kid told her how awesome the UDM act had been. Grown-ups, too!

Ms. Starr couldn't stop beaming. "Yes, such amazing students!"

She gestured for Pepper to draw closer. When Pepper did, the teacher smiled playfully and opened her unusually large pocketbook.

"You did very well controlling your fiercing under pressure," Carrot said from within. She was nestled on a blanket and wearing a bow around her neck for the occasion. "And it goes without saying that your percussion was just beautiful."

"Carrot, have you been crying?" Pepper asked.

Carrot huffed. "Crying? Me? Absolutely not!" Then her enormous eyes welled with tears right there in front of Pepper, and she swiped at them with her paw. "Maybe just a bit. It was very moving. Much better than the American Rabbit Breeders' Annual Competition."

Pepper's sister, Taffy, barreled into her. Next came Graham and Jam. Then her parents.

"Honey, that was spectacular," said Pepper's mom.

"We're so proud," said Pepper's dad.

Mrs. Winterbottom came over next. "You were wonderful!" she gushed. "And you played 'Crazy-Daisy Shame'!"

"You know Everyday Cake?" asked Pepper, surprised.

"Sure, they're my favorite band," said Mrs. Winterbottom, winking.

"You're a star, Pep-Pep!" Taffy said. She wrinkled her brows into a sweet little knot. "But where's Zinnia? I saw Violet, but not Zinnia."

Zinnia! Pepper clapped her hand to her head. "I've got to run," she told her family. "Love you so much. I'll be back in a minute!"

She ran out of the reception and down the hall. "Zinnia!" she called as she jogged. "Zinnia?"

Zinnia wasn't in the UDM classroom.

She wasn't in the fifth-grade Flares' room, either.

Or the Flare lab.

Or the bathroom.

Where was she?

Then Pepper tried the supply closet. Her hide-out. Nory's hideout. The hideout she'd shared with only Carrot and Ms. Starr.

It was dark in the closet. Darker than usual, because the lights were off in the hallway. Pepper had never been to the closet at night. She fumbled for the light switch, but before she found it, she heard a scratchy sound. Zinnia held up a rolled piece of paper, the end of which burned brightly.

"I come in here to hide out sometimes," Zinnia said. "To get away from Lacey, or just to think."

Pepper flipped on the light, and Zinnia blew out her flaming paper.

"I come in here, too," said Pepper.

"Really?"

"Yeah." Pepper reached up to the back of a shelf and pulled out a half-empty bag of choco fire trucks. "See? I have a candy stash."

"Wow." Zinnia held out her hand and Pepper shook some trucks into it, then took some for herself.

"I'm sorry I said all those things," Pepper said.

"It's okay," Zinnia said. "I know how it must have looked. But just so you know, I was never a spy."

"I know that now. Elliott and Nory told me everything."

"I just wanted to help. I was so nervous with everyone watching me warm the instruments that I overdid it. Most people underflare when they're learning, but I overflare, which is much more dangerous. I'm glad no one got hurt."

"I should have trusted you. But with magic like mine, I've gotten used to people not wanting me around. So it was easy to believe you weren't really my friend."

"I get it."

"Thanks," Pepper said.

"And I understand why you thought what you thought, after everything I did earlier this year." Zinnia chewed on her lip. "Anyway. How did it go? Your number? I bet you rocked it."

Pepper slid her back along the wall and sat beside her. "We rocked it," she said. "Elliott made icicles that I could use for percussion and Nory turned into a kittingo at the end."

"That's great."

Pepper jiggled Zinnia's arm. "Thanks for talking me out of being so nervous."

"No problem."

"Come out, okay?" Pepper said. "Taffy's asking for you, and they're announcing the winners at the end of the reception."

Zinnia stood. She grabbed Pepper's hand and pulled her up, too.

Nory still hadn't seen Father, Hawthorn, or Dalia. When the performance had ended, her main worry was Piano-Bax. She knew that he still couldn't turn himself back.

First thing was to help Nurse Riley wheel Piano-Bax down to the nurse's office. Then she'd dragged Coach to the nurse's to help with post-fluxing nutrition. Nory finally arrived back at the hall while the reception was still in full swing.

"Do you want some punch?" Ms. Starr said, appearing behind Nory as she hovered at the edge of the crowd. "I'd love to meet your father."

They found Father, Hawthorn, and Dalia sitting near the front of the auditorium. Dalia leapt up and hugged Nory.

"You guys sounded great!" Dalia exclaimed.

It wasn't quite the same as her saying *Your kittingo was great*, but Nory hugged her sister back.

Hawthorn hugged Nory, too. He and Dalia were dressed up. He was in a suit jacket and tie. Dalia had on a knee-length dress with a white collar. Father was wearing his second-best suit.

"I loved seeing you with your friends," Hawthorn said. "I'm so glad you found such good people here."

That *also* wasn't quite the same as *Your kittingo was great*, but Nory hugged Hawthorn back, too. "I'm glad you came," she told them.

"We got lost," said Hawthorn. "Just ask Aunt Margo if you want proof. We texted her four times because we were driving around, trying to find the school. There's something weird with the address. Artichoke Avenue. Artichoke Street. It turns out they're not the same."

"Father got lost?" Nory almost couldn't believe it was true.

She turned to face Father. Suddenly her jeans and purple T-shirt seemed like the wrong things to be wearing. Her hair felt big and out of control. "Father," she said, pasting on a smile. "Thank you for coming to my show. It's good to see you. May I introduce my teacher, Ms. Starr? Ms. Starr, this is my father, Dr. Stone Horace."

Father reached out and shook Ms. Starr's hand first, then Nory's. "I'm glad to see you looking so healthy," he said.

"Thank you for the rain boots."

"You're welcome. Is there anything else you need for the winter? I'll have your cold-weather clothes sent over and give Margo some funds to take you shopping. You look like you've grown."

"You must be extremely proud of Nory," Ms. Starr put in, placing her arm around Nory's shoulders.

"Well," he said, "I don't use the word *proud* lightly."

Nory wanted to hide her face just then. But Ms. Starr pressed on. "Have you considered admitting Upside-Down Magic students to Sage Academy?" she asked Father. "The program is new and could use public support from well-known educators like yourself. Lots of school districts are thinking about creating UDM classrooms, but many haven't done it yet."

Nory's father looked flustered. Then he puffed out his chest and cleared his throat. "Ms. Starr, I'm glad Nory's getting an education here, and I still have hopes that it will help her. What I saw tonight suggests that she's still not capable of traditional fluxing for more than a couple seconds."

"The kittingo was on purpose, Father!" said Nory.

Father arched his eyebrows.

"It was. Truly!" said Nory. "I could have stayed a flamingo, but I wanted to . . . I wanted to show everyone . . ." Her voice trailed off.

When Father said nothing, Ms. Starr said, "Ah. I didn't realize."

"You didn't realize what?" Nory's father said.

"That you were a small-minded man," said Ms. Starr. "I suppose I won't change your mind, then. Small minds are often unable to make turnarounds. I'm glad Nory didn't inherit *that* from you."

Nory gasped.

Father just stared.

Ms. Starr drew herself up. "Good-bye, Dr. Horace." She walked back toward the stage.

Nory turned toward her family. "Thank you for coming," she said. Then she hugged Hawthorn and Dalia—and followed Ms. Starr.

Yes, Nory walked away from Father, away from her brother and sister, and went instead with Ms. Starr.

It was a hard thing to do. But it felt right.

The auditorium was full. Principal Gonzalez made the announcements. Nory stood at the back with her teacher.

"Let's start with the eighth grade. First place goes to the Flyers!"

The eighth-grade Flyers cheered. Then they all raised themselves a foot off the ground and pumped their arms in the air. They had staged a human circus for their act and had flown from pretend cannons.

The Flickers won seventh grade. Their act had involved ladders and a live tic-tac-toe match. The Flickers were dressed in X-and-O sweaters and appeared with each move.

The Fuzzies won sixth grade. Their act involved fifteen groundhogs who'd actually listened to them. The groundhogs had made a pyramid.

Principal Gonzalez paused for effect. "And the fifth-grade winners of the Dunwiddle Show Off are . . ." There was a drumroll. "The fifth-grade Flares!"

Nory's heart sank.

Boo. Drat.

The Sparkies had won.

They *had* been pretty amazing . . .

But still. They were Sparkies.

"And now," Principal Gonzales said, "the prize for Most Original Show Off—for the entire school—goes to . . ."

Nory held her breath.

"The fifth-grade Upside-Down Magic class!"

Hooray!

Everyone in UDM cried and hugged one another.

Except Bax, who was still in the nurse's office. He was no longer a piano and well on the way to recovery, but still feeling a little off-key.

After the ceremony, everyone went out on the lawn in front of the school. Hawthorn and Dalia found Nory and came over.

"I miss you," said Dalia, squashing Nory in her arms. "I wish you could come home."

"I miss you, too," said Hawthorn.

Nory stole a glance at Father, who was checking his phone. He wore an expression she'd never seen on him before: shame.

"I think I *am* home," she said. She watched their faces to see if they understood. "But I miss you, too. Maybe you can come stay with us for a weekend sometime."

"That would be fun," Hawthorn said.

"Would we eat Fruity Doodles for breakfast?" Dalia asked.

"You can eat them straight out of the box," said Nory.

She said good-bye and went to find Aunt Margo and Figs.

Her aunt squealed when she saw her. "Nory! That was incredible. That was beyond incredible. You are amazing. Such style!"

"Flamingo, huh, kid?" Figs said, patting her shoulder. "I could never get my birds to go right. Never. Always had trouble with the beak, even in my high-school Bird Intensive. Well done."

"Thanks," she said.

"I think we should go for a celebratory ice cream,"

Aunt Margo said. "Do you want to ask your friends to join us?"

"Yes," Nory said. "I'd love that."

So Nory, Figs, and Margo went to the sweet shop with Elliott's family, Bax and his dad, Marigold and her grandparents, Pepper and her enormous family, and even Coach (who didn't eat ice cream but drank a peppermint tea). They filled up the whole shop, and got double scoops of ice cream, and everyone was loud and happy. Elliott refroze the ice creams when they started to melt.

19

Mrs. Winterbottom, Pepper's first pest-removal customer, had two sons and one daughter. The sons were Flyers and had grown up and moved away to become lawyers. The daughter, on the other hand, was a Flicker. She'd pursued a different path. An unusual path. One might even say a *wonky* path. It was a path many people worried was a waste of time.

It wasn't.

In fact, Pepper thought, Arabelle Pumpkin Winterbottom sounded even more amazing in person than on recordings. Her voice was like the ringing of the strongest triangle. As the lead singer of Everyday Cake, she had bright blue hair and charisma that won over everyone in the packed stadium.

Especially the kids in the special VIP section.

They all had seats, but most of them were standing up. Elliott played the air guitar. Sebastian wore both his head cone and his blindfold. He stood quietly, waving an imaginary baton as he listened without looking. Andres wore a backpack full of bricks, and beat rhythms on his seat with his hands. Willa and Marigold danced with Zinnia and Pepper. Not interpretive dance, just regular dance. Bax did a knee-bending, jiggling thing that he said was definitely not dancing.

Nory sang her head off. No one could hear her over the music, and it felt good to sing without people judging.

Mrs. Winterbottom had seen Upside-Down Magic in the Show Off. She was thrilled that they'd performed an Everyday Cake song. The very next day, she had given Pepper ten VIP passes. One for each UDM kid, one for Mr. Phan, and one for Zinnia.

The first notes of "Crazy-Daisy Shame" started to play. Everybody screamed in excitement.

Nory, Pepper, and their friends all began to sing the first verse, at top volume, along with the band:

> *If you've given me up,*
> *I'll be okay without you!*
> *I am one of a kind*
> *And I've got my crew.*
> *It's true, I'm one of a kind*
> *And I've got my crew.*

Nory had heard these words hundreds of times before.

But now?

She truly knew what they meant.

Nory, Andres, and friends return for another

upside-down adventure in:

UPSIDE★DOWN MAGIC #4: DRAGON OVERNIGHT

About the Authors

SARAH MLYNOWSKI is the author of many books for tweens, teens, and adults, including the *New York Times* bestselling Whatever After series, the Magic in Manhattan series, and *Gimme a Call*. She would like to be a Flicker so she could make the mess in her room invisible. Visit her online at www.sarahm.com.

LAUREN MYRACLE is the *New York Times* bestselling author of many books for young readers, including The Winnie Years series, the Flower Power series, the Life of Ty series, and the Wishing Day series, which starts with the book *Wishing Day*. She would like to be a Fuzzy so she could talk to unicorns and feed them berries. You can find Lauren online at www.laurenmyracle.com.

EMILY JENKINS is the author of many chapter books, including the Toys trilogy (which begins with *Toys Go Out*) and the Invisible Inkling series. Her picture books include *Toys Meet Snow, Princessland,* and *A Greyhound, a Groundhog.* She would like to be a Flare and work as a pastry chef. Visit Emily at www.emilyjenkins.com.